ILLUMINATI

DECEMBER 21

"...All these things will I give thee, if thou wilt fall
down and worship me" – Matthew 4:9

Publisher's Cataloging in Publication Data

©2009 by Nishan A. Kumaraperu,1974
Illuminati-2012
LCCN: 2009900197
ISBN: 978-0-615-27176-7
Science Fiction, Suspense, Fantasy, Action Adventure
PS648.S3
813
Published By: Nishan A. Kumaraperu

A work of fiction...*or is it*?

WWW.MORNINGSON.INFO

CHAPTER 1: IT BEGINS

BOSTON - JANUARY 6TH, 2011 -

Thirty miles, on the southwest end of the city, an immense building loomed in the distant skyline. It rose up among the smaller ones like a King amidst his paupers.

A lone man sat at an immense mahogany office desk, barely silhouetted in the light of the last remaining rays of sunset. It was dark in the room, but that did not belie the fact that the office was large and spacious. Works of art by prominent artists hung on the beige colored walls.

A large bay window, usually opening up to the lights of the city stood partially covered by expensive Venetian blinds. It looked like the typical office of a top executive; except for the red and black candles, arranged in a unique star shape that aligned the floor of the room.

The man in the shadows waited patiently as if in deep thought; his suit-covered arms, the only sign that someone was behind the desk. He sat there in the dark, rubbing a black crucifix between his thumb and fore finger. He reached his hand down and pushed a button on the glimmering silver intercom. A course voice answered on the other end.

"Yes?"

"**It's time**," he said simply, and cut off the intercom

WUSHU ACADEMY, BRECK BAY -

The crowd was cheering as the two young men went after each other in a flurry of fists. To Ethan, this was pure adrenaline unleashed; man-to-man fighting at its most primitive. He had always been a risk-taker: skydiving, deep-sea diving, mountain-climbing; anything to raise the blood pressure.

WuShu was a Chinese martial art he had been involved in since grade school. Literally translated, "Wu" is military, "Shu" is art; the art of fighting. The difficulty factor alone set WuShu apart from other forms of martial arts.

He had been a trouble-maker as a kid and his Father had forced him into joining Martial Arts as a way to keep him disciplined and focused. He had hated it at first; the thought of being forced to do something he did not want to do. He had considered himself a pacifist before this, but had reluctantly attended the Academy.

Throughout the years, he had begun to find out that he was a very quick learner and had quite an aptitude for it. Ethan discovered early on in life, that he had a photographic memory. He could remember everything he put his mind to and recall most anything. He memorized WuShu forms and applications at such an accelerated rate that he soon became his teacher's best student.

In fact, he was so proficient in Wushu that he had incorporated multiple fighting styles into what he already knew: Kung Fu; Silat; Kenpo; and Akaido. He found the graceful acrobatics and violent applications of these styles quite exhilarating.

The roar from the crowd that had gathered around him brought him back into focus, elevating his confidence; he loved the sound of encouragement from them. Then again, he liked to fight. He was very good at it.

Ethan blocked a jab and came in with a quick kick to his opponent's shins. The tall muscular man recovered quickly and pushed in with a roundhouse kick towards Ethan's head. Ducking, Ethan grabbed the other man's leg, hit it with a powerful fist and brought him down.

The other man grimaced in pain and fell to the ground. He took Ethan's outstretched hand and pulled himself back up, breathing hard.

"Good fight; Damn you hit hard", said Malcolm.

"Next time, Malcolm; you're getting better."

Both men slapped hands and Ethan walked away from the crowd and back to the locker room.

Ethan was in great shape, a strong, muscular physique to match an ideal height and weight. He had been told he was rather handsome and his confident personality reflected this. He grabbed a quick shower, got dressed, and hurried out to his car.

SWATHMORE UNIVERSITY – LECTURE CENTER -

Ethan Swan's main love was for Archeology; his minor being Political Science. He became interested in the subject from his Father, Earl Swan. Professor Swan had raised Ethan in the interpretation of archaic documents, symbols, and history from birth.

Swan had gone on to become famous due to his views on political and social reform, as well as unique archeological finds. Two years ago, Dr. Swan was killed in an automobile accident; until then, he hadn't seen his father for almost three years.

It wasn't that he did not *want* to see him; but his father was constantly on archeology digs and other business meetings around the world. Between his schedule and his father's, time was scarce. Besides that, he had not been terribly close with his father.

Earl Swan had always kept Ethan at a distance; but at the same time, had always managed to be there for him when the need arose. The funeral had been hard to handle; more so, because of the wasted time between them. Ethan had been devastated and always felt guilty for not trying harder for a closer relationship.

Swathmore University, on the other hand, was a place where Ethan felt at home and could keep his attention focused away from the pain of his father's death.

The University had a long-standing world-wide reputation not only for excellence in academic research, but its innovative benefits to society. It was a very large University, consisting of multiple faculties spread across two campuses, uniquely combining the liberal arts with exceptional professional programs.

The Professors at Swathmore were dedicated to their pursuit of knowledge and the education of their students. Ethan's courses were sparse, but advanced because of his great aptitude for learning. He very much enjoyed the days spent here.

His Professor, Doctor Winehouse had become a close friend and confidant over the last four years. After his father's death, Professor Winehouse had helped Ethan cope with the tragedy.

The Professor was amicable and had a great sense of humor. He reminded Ethan of Albert Einstein; mostly due to his wild grey hair sticking up from his head. Of course, the man was undoubtedly brilliant and a highly skilled public speaker. He was a caring old man and Ethan respected him immensely for all his help and support he had given him.

Ethan approached the lecture hall and saw that the auditorium was filled to capacity. The conference center was elegant in the literal sense of the word. The inlaid marble tile ran the expanse of the high-vaulted walls. Seating was spacious; enough for a very large crowd. Their high-quality black commercial fabric stood out in the lighted auditorium like the dotted modules of a circuit board. An immense crystal chandelier hung downwards from the ornate ceiling. It was an incredibly beautiful place.

Trying to find room, he finally picked a place to stand in the back corner. Doctor Phillip Winehouse was already lecturing to a gathered crowd of intellects.

"….As I was saying, the Knights Templar began in 1120 AD, as a band of modest monks. At this time, they were the protectors of the people of Jerusalem. As they gained in power and notoriety, their convictions began to change; their Christian faith had given way to secret occultist rituals and black magic. Some say they turned away from God due to their betrayal by the Catholic Church. That of course, is *a story in itself,*"

Doctor Winehouse paused for a minute as he surveyed the crowd. He did not want to offend those that considered their religion sacred. But the fact remained, unsaid as it may be.

The Templars' existence was tied closely to the Crusades and when the Holy Land was lost, the Church's support for their order faded. The Templars had been betrayed by the very organization that had created them. To that end, their anger turned to distrust and hate for all things Christian.

He cleared his throat before he continued with his tirade.

"The Templars infiltrated the fraternity known as Freemasonry, adapting and altering the sect to accommodate the Templars' own philosophy, beliefs, and occultist rituals. Later still, freemasonry was further perverted by a Civil War General by the name of Albert Pike; who by the way was also a top leader in the Ku Klux Klan. Pike was said to be a Satanist, who deeply *indulged* in the occult.

Pike's future design was one of world conquest through three world wars; essentially bringing about the New World Order. This *'New World*

Order' became the mantra for the Illuminati of today, which I might also add, was *founded* by Ignatius De Loyola, a *Roman Catholic Jesuit*! The Vatican has kept this fact under wraps for quite some time. Sometime after that, a man named Adam Weishaupt brought the Illuminati towards its more traditional and satanic values. As some may believe, the *reckoning of man* is now set to unfold. Any questions before I move on?"

A beautiful young woman from the crowd stood up from her seat. "Doctor Winehouse, what exactly *do you believe the* Illuminati are?"

Winehouse stared at her for a moment too long and smiled. She was striking indeed. At his age, however, she would not have looked at him twice if he had not been up at the podium. What a shame he had let the pursuit of knowledge overshadow his need for love. If only he were ten years younger. He sighed deeply before he began again.

"*That* is a very good question, my dear. For those here, who do not know, the more *modern* Illuminati was first formed as a no-name group to challenge Roman Catholic Authority by

Adam Weishaupt; *also a Jesuit* and a professor of Canon Law.

He believed that there were only a few among us destined for 'Enlightenment'; chosen to guide and *rule the world*. Weishaupt and his associates infiltrated many lodges and orders; such as the Freemasons, gaining followers, sympathetic to his cause. The group gradually became an openly destructive Luciferian cult and grew into one of the most feared & powerful shadow governments in history, taking on the name: *Illuminati*."

Weishaupt surveyed the crowd as he spoke. As he was when he had first discovered the truth, the people were awed as to the origin of the Illuminati. Who would ever have thought that this cult had been birthed through a perverted twisting of the Catholic faith.

"Either way, the goal of the Illuminati is simple and has been in progression for centuries: to create a one-world government, a one-world religion, and a one-world currency. This would, in effect, give them the absolute power to literally rule this world.

Their god is Lucifer and by using their wealth, occult practices, and positions of power, they can manipulate & influence the masses of the world!"

"Thank you Professor, but isn't that going a little too far?" interrupted the young woman, "I mean you're talking as if these people are trying to *take over the world*!"

She looked visibly irritated as she stared back at Whinehouse, as if daring him to continue. The Professor had always been confident in his research and beliefs and was not swayed easily.

"No Miss, I strongly believe that the majority of this world's population is being manipulated into exactly what these people want us to do, think, & feel!"

The Professor paused for a minute and looked at the woman inquiringly.

"What is your name Miss? If you would like to discuss this further, I suggest you see me after the lecture; my time is almost up."

She flashed him a strange smirk as if she was relieved at what he had suggested. She absently adjusted the back of her blouse as she spoke.

"It's Samantha Turner; and I would love to. Thank you, please continue."

"It would be my pleasure, Ms. Turner. I would like to conclude with the present structure of the Illuminati today. Their highly organized operation is composed of the richest of the rich; 13 families who have been deeply involved for generations. They call themselves De Gilderberg Group. This organization has been charged with the post-war takeover of the democratic process. Measures implemented by this group provide proof that they have already taken over partial control of the world economy through indirect political means.

To this end, it seems they already control the fluctuations of world currency, the media; and through the media – what we are led to think and believe. "

Doctor Winehouse paused and glanced down at his watch. He was looking forward to spend some time with the lovely Ms. Turner.

"It seems I am out of time. Thank you all for coming & I appreciate the opportunity to speak to you today."

As Doctor Winehouse walked out of the
conference hall, hushed whispers were heard
amongst some audience members. Ethan waited
until the crowd cleared & left as well to catch up
with Winehouse.

The 'Great Hall', as some had named it, was
close to a hundred yards long. Works of art
hung along the walls and exquisite marble tile
lined the floors. It led to the offices of the
distinguished professors who taught at
Swathmore University. The hall was empty, as
most of the attendee's had left. Doctor
Winehouse's spacious quarters were at the far
end of the Hall.

Walking along, Ethan made out two figures
talking to each other. One was distinctly Doctor
Winehouse; the other, he also recognized as the
young woman at the lecture hall. She was
gorgeous, yet had looked very distinguished &
dressed professionally. Her long red hair fell
down her pale skin like a fountain of blood. He
remembered her name as being Samantha
Turner. They turned to enter Winehouse's office.

"Hey Doc, wait up," Ethan called.

Doctor Winehouse turned his friendly looking face with a smile, recognizing Ethan's voice. He nodded his head towards him. At the same instant, the woman, known as Samantha Turner grabbed him by the hair, pulled his head back, and slit his throat with a very large knife.

Blood spurted forth from his lacerated throat. Winehouse gurgled uncontrollably, trying to voice words he could not. He reached a hand to his throat, frantically trying to stop the flow. The next minute, he hit the ground face first, with a thud that almost brought Ethan to his knees.

In utter shock & anguish, Ethan started running towards them, yet instinctively knowing how he was going to disarm her. Everything seemed to be happening in slow motion. The woman turned towards him and ripped open her blouse; buttons bursting from the expensive cloth. An eye with rays of light spewing forth was inscribed on her naked body. She looked at him and laughed as she brought the knife down into her own tattooed chest.

Ethan finally reached her, executing a leg sweep and bringing her down to the ground. He straddled her with his knees, forcing her arms apart. He grabbed her by both arms, shaking her violently.

"WHY," he screamed at her, "He was like a Father to me! WHO are you?! My God, What have you done?!"

She looked into his eyes, with what actually looked like lust. "God...has nothing to do...with this," she coughed, as her eyes rolled back into her head. She died with a smile on her face, as if she were in ecstasy.

Wracked with sobs, Ethan checked her pulse, and then stumbled over to where Doctor Winehouse was sprawled, in a puddle of blood. His vacant eyes stared outward into space; a large gash on his throat spilled out his remaining life force. Ethan touched him lovingly on his cheek and closed his eyes for the final time.

"I'm so sorry Doc...' Ethan spoke to no one in particular. His head was spinning; he felt weak in the knees and fell down. He could not believe what had just happened. He took a few deep breaths before he took control of himself.

After what seemed like an eternity, Ethan wiped the wetness from his eyes and forced himself to stand up. He tried not to look at the knife buried in the woman's chest. To no avail, that was exactly where his gaze fell…and lingered.

The shape and uniqueness of the blade looked disturbingly familiar. He had seen something like it before. Upon closer inspection, he understood from where that was. He forced himself, step by step, into Winehouse's office and dialed 911 on the telephone.

"911 Emergency…"

Ethan did his best to relay what had just taken place in the 'Great Hall' at Swathmore University. Strangely, he did not falter with his words. The operator told him to wait there until help arrived.

As he sat waiting for the police to come, he caught a glimpse, just for a second, of something jutting out of the woman's hand. Yes, there it was - It looked to have been imbedded into her skin, like a splinter. Using a pair of tweezers he found on the Professor's desk, he carefully pulled it from her palm.

It looked like a very tiny sliver of metal with markings, like some type of code written on it. Perhaps a circuit or microchip of some sort; if so, what the hell was it doing in embedded into someone's skin?

He heard the police sirens and promptly placed it in one of Professor Winehouse's scattered sample bags & then into his jacket pocket. The door at the far end of the hall opened and a small army of police officers walked in. A large man in an expensive suit stepped briskly in front of the others and approached Ethan.

"We'll have some questions for you," he stated as he walked past him, towards the bodies. The big-boned man bent down and appeared to be taking a pulse and then searching the woman for some kind of identification.

The others continued to carry on with the crime scene investigation for what seemed like hours. Meanwhile, one of the other officers proceeded to question Ethan. Explaining as best he could of the strange events that had taken place, Ethan finally broke down.

"He was a good man; he was my *friend*! Why would someone do this?! *Who* is she?!"

"Calm down Mr. Swan", said Officer Towns, "we're doing our best. You mentioned something about the knife?"

Officer Towns was a burly man whose skin was as pale as the moon's. He appeared as if he had stepped out of a recruitment poster; his uniform neatly pressed and tucked in and everything about him in order to perfection. His steely gaze as he stared at Ethan gave the impression that he was being considered a suspect.

"It's called a Khukuri Knife; the blades are long and curved like that for maximum effect," Ethan explained, "You didn't answer my question; who the hell is that woman and why would she kill the Professor?!"

Officer Towns looked irritated as he shook his head and sighed.

"*That* is what we are trying to figure out, son. She has no I.D. on her; no one has seen her around here before. I have a feeling that a fingerprint analysis is going to be useless. The forensic analyst says that the fingerprints have been filed off. We are sending her picture to be run through the FBI database, but the results will take some time."

"So, you're telling me that nobody knows who she is or where she came from?! What kind of…"

Ethan felt exhausted and angry. He looked back at the officer. No one had ever died at his feet before; he had no idea what to do. In fact, the only thought he had was that he was going to be sick.

"Look; I need to get out of here. I need some time away from all of this!"

"I understand. We've got all your information. We'll be in touch."

Ethan composed himself and walked back over to look at the Professor one last time. He silently said his goodbyes and headed out of the office. As he was passing by, he overheard Officer Towns conversing with a small group. A plain clothes officer turned his head to look over at him, then back to the group.

"Is that all he said? Just what the hell is a Kookroo knife? How the hell is that gonna help us?!"

"It should," Ethan stated, as he approached, "A Khukuri Knife is used by old-world tribes and cults alike; *that* should be your starting point."

"*Used*," the officer asked sarcastically, "Used for what kid?"

"...*Used* for Ritual Sacrifice."

Ethan walked out of the room and out of the University. The fresh air was a Heaven-sent after being stuck in a room that had reeked of death. He was surprised that he was keeping it together so well with the recent events. He headed towards the parking lot, got into his car, and then drove to his condo.

The upper west side of Boston was known for its thriving commercial districts, vibrant centers of commerce, and its unique and cultural neighborhoods. Ethan's condo was in Breck Bay, a higher-class section of the city. Ethan had been awarded a very large trust fund by his godfather, Christoph Natash upon his Father's death.

Christoph was a German Scientist who had been a close family friend every since Ethan could remember. He was a genius in genetics and seemed to know everyone, both domestically and afar. Natash had helped Ethan pick out the condo in Breck Bay about 8 months back.

Ethan had a fancy for the high-life. Nice places, fast cars, good food, and so on. He chose a grand looking condo in a tall building called

Cypress Terrace. The place had a modern setup, fully furnished, and even a pre-installed mini bar. He drove a BMW M5; a top of the line sedan with a V10 500 Horsepower engine. He loved to cook, but preferred, as most young bachelors do, to live solely on take-out pizza.

Ethan took the elevator up to the 3rd floor and walked up to his door. As he was punching his key code into the electronic pad, the door opened across the hall and a gorgeous older woman stepped out in her red silk robe.

Cassie Parker was his neighbor; a beautiful divorced woman in her late 30's. She was what was known as a 'cougar'; always on the prowl for younger men. Ethan and she had a unique bedroom relationship.

They had met a few times while passing each other in the building. He remembered that she had initiated the first conversation on the elevator, going down to the parking garage. Things had progressed from there and before he knew it, they were having sex on and off.

Cassie was a strange one all right, who always kept to herself. In fact, he had never seen her with any friends or family since he had known her. She had always been respectful of his privacy and never pried into his personal life; he was grateful for that. He had always assumed that she was a lonely widow who had recently just lost her husband. God only knew why a woman such as her would choose to be alone.

"Hey there sexy, I'm glad your finally home", she growled, "I haven't seen you here for 3 days! Why don't you come on in for a minute?"

Staring at her long legs peeking out of the robe, Ethan almost considered it. His mind, however, was on other things at the moment. The only comfort he wanted was to be alone.

"I'm *really* not in the mood Cassie", Ethan replied, "I'm going to my place tonight."

"Where the hell have you been," she insisted.

"It doesn't matter; we can talk later, alright?"

"Come on Ethan; I'm feeling a bit *kinky* tonight! How about I change your mind? What time do you want to get together?"

Ethan shook his head in irritation. It seemed that the only thing this woman ever thought about was how to get him into her bed. He didn't want to do that and he damned well did not want to explain what had happened to him this night. He wanted to forget.

"How about *never* Cassie; is never a good time for you," he replied sarcastically, "stop being such a pushy bitch!"

"Asshole," she screamed, as she began to shut the door.

She opened it back up a crack and threw something at him. It bounced off the door and onto the floor.

"*Here*; it came for you 2 days ago", she yelled before slamming the door in his face.

He reached down and picked up the parcel. It was a package wrapped in plain brown paper.

Ethan walked into his condo and tossed his car keys onto the counter. He fell down into his Beansac, a piece of alternative furniture shaped like a beanbag. The day had been draining and he was exhausted. He could not get his thoughts off of Doctor Winehouse.

The Professor had been like a Father to him since Ethan had first come to Swathmore

University. Winehouse had taken an instant liking to Ethan and vice versa; they had started off immediately as friends and confidants.

He remembered the many times they had discussed politics, religion, conspiracy theory, and life in general. They had spent many a long night debating on multiple religious and social issues. Ethan felt a great sadness, but strangely, not frightened anymore about the events that had transpired today. He more so felt an obligation to Winehouse to find out *why* he was murdered.

Ethan walked into the bathroom, undressed, and got into the shower. He needed to reinvigorate himself. The sound of the water was soothing and relaxing. As the beat of the droplets came down, he felt himself drift.

He was drowning! At least it felt like he was. It was dark; horribly dark. He pounded against the cold grey exterior of his 'cage'; a dull metallic sound his only response. There was no discernable exit from whatever he was trapped in. His breathing was erratic and his heart felt like it would explode; he screamed!

His eyes snapped open to the sound of knocking. He didn't know how long he had been in the shower, but it had felt like an eternity. The knocking came again. Someone was at his door.

Ethan got out of the shower and wrapped a towel around him. He glanced at the fancy alarm clock above the dresser; it was close to midnight. Who the hell was here at this time of night, he thought to himself. The knocking was louder this time. He ran to the door, half expecting it to be Cassie Parker again.

"Yeah, who is it?"

"Detective Samael, Mr. Swan. We met earlier today."

What's wrong with these cops, Ethan thought, don't they respect a person's right to sleep.

"Can this wait until tomorrow, Detective?"

"I have some more questions for you regarding the incident today. I'm sorry; it can't wait until morning."

Sighing, Ethan opened the door and let him in. It was the large man in the ritzy suit from earlier that day. The detective completely ignored Ethan as he stepped through the doorway, all the while looking up and down the apartment. He walked right in and took a seat on Ethan's favorite chair, the Beansac. What an asshole!

The man was about 6 foot 5, looked to be about in his mid-50's. His expensive suit clashed with his worn leather shoes. His face was handsome and chiseled, but his eyes looked cold and vacant. The small notepad he had taken out had a picture of a pyramid on it. Ethan always seemed to notice all the finer details about the people he met. It was almost instinctual. Samael just sat there looking at him, not saying a word.

"What can I do for you detective?" Ethan prompted, "It's late."

"I need answers," Samael stated. He was being very forward.

"What do you want," Ethan pushed.

"You left in quite a hurry, kid. Was there something more important you had to do than helping us with this investigation?"

Ethan remained silent as he stared hard at the man. The detective ignored him as he continued.

"I need to know about the knife we found in the dead woman. How is it that you know so much about what its purpose was for?"

Ethan began to pace about the room. What kind of question was that, he thought to himself. He sure was rather blunt about all of this.

"My father was a Professor of Archeology; he taught me everything he knew, including ancient customs and the tools they used."

Ethan paused, taking it all in.

"Am I being considered a *suspect*?"

The Detective scribbled something in his notebook. He rubbed his chin thoughtfully.

"Mr. Swan; I am aware that you possess a genius level intellect, considerable skill in the martial arts, and obviously an interest in ancient weapons."

Ethan looked at him in anger. They thought he killed Winehouse! This was an obvious attempt to get him to stumble upon his words and say something they could hold against him.

"What the hell are you getting at?"

"Relax Kid; I already know you and Winehouse were close; we searched his home. Your fingerprints were all over his house."

"He was a good friend," Ethan stated, "I was over many times; *of course*, my fingerprints would be there!"

"That's not what concerns me," pressed Samael.

"Then get to the *damn point* Detective!"

The detective looked at him angrily and then reached into his jacket pocket.

"We found a partially written letter with your name on it. Take a look."

Detective Samael produced a small plastic bag with a letter enclosed in it. He handed it to Ethan. It was in Winehouse's handwriting.

My Dear Ethan Swan;

I should *despise* you for what you represent, however I cannot. It is no fault of yours; you did not *ask* for this. We have become very close; you and I. I have this bizarre feeling that this may be the last time we speak. The ways of the world have become twisted & perverse but I have come to believe that human beings will always have a choice in doing what is right.

What I am about to tell you may seem like fiction; but I assure you, I have found the necessary proof. I should have every reason to doubt your intentions, but…….

Ethan maintained his composure and handed the letter back to Samael. Sadness filled his heart. The letter had ended abruptly. Something had obviously kept Winehouse from finishing.

"I…I don't understand why he would write this. He was…my friend."

The detective was looking at him suspiciously. His lips curled in a twisted grin.

"Are you sure this doesn't *mean* anything to you?"

"I don't know what you are talking about; what do you mean," Ethan replied frantically.

"Do you remember *anything D114?*"

Ethan suddenly felt faint. His eyes glazed over as everything went black.

He was in, what looked like a small, dark room. Red and black candles were the only source of light. People in lab coats were taking readings from a small machine attached to his arm. He saw himself in a first-person point of view, but noticed that his arms were small and skinny; he was just a kid! Others dressed in masks resembling the heads of goats were chanting unintelligibly. A large black Pentagram was drawn on the immaculately clean tile floor. The scene slowly faded like a dying rainbow.

He came to with a throbbing pain in his head. It felt like cold metal was grinding down on his skull. He slowly opened his eyes. Detective Samael was looking at him with those cold dead eyes, speaking, but the words coming out incoherently. A smile spread across his face showing the glint of sharply filed teeth. Things came into focus slowly. The large man had removed his shirt; intricate occultist tattoos spread about his muscled body. Ethan could make out a few words here and there.

"…not ready…"

"…tell me…what…know."

"…blood will be spilled."

Ethan concentrated and the spinning stopped. The room was a mess. Files and documents had been thrown all over the floor, furniture had been pushed over; glass was broken. A 357 Magnum Revolver was pushed against his head. Detective Samael was staring down at him, that stupid smile still on his face. Ethan took all of this in within a span of 3 seconds.

"I'm afraid Ms. Turner could not *finish* the job; I on the other hand…"

He heard the hammer of the revolver being cocked. Instinctively, Ethan snapped his head to the side and hit the barrel of the gun, turning it away from him. Using his other hand to grab hold of the butt, he pulled downward. Samael fell forward. The full force of his knee caught Samael underneath the jaw as a calculated elbow slammed into the side of his head. Upright now, Ethan grabbed the detective by his hair and twisted him around until he had him by the throat.

"Who the hell *are* you? What do your want with *me*?"

The detective didn't say a word. Ethan put more pressure on his throat.

"You know; my life seems to be spiraling right into the toilet. Why would a **cop** want to **kill** me? Answer me!" he spat at Samael.

Samael laughed hoarsely.

"You *must* die. You are *not* ready!"

"I'll repeat myself *one* time; that's it. *Who* are you?"

"It's too *soon*." the detective stated.

Samael threw his neck back, colliding with Ethan's face. He grabbed the gun from Ethan's hand, put it into his mouth, and pulled the trigger. Brain matter sprayed the room with splatters of crimson. Samael fell to the ground with a loud thud.

Ethan opened his mouth in shock and disgust, but no words came forth. What the hell had just happened?! He was breathing heavily, but recovered quickly. This was the second suicide he had witnessed in one day. Who were these people? What could possess someone to do something like this? Why or how was *he* involved? Questions were clouding his mind. He needed answers.

He approached Samael's body. Trying not to look at what was left of his head, he quickly began to scan the detective's chest. In the center of his torso, was a skull with diagonal bones; the arms were lined with tribal designs used by the ancient Mayan civilization.

Ethan knew exactly what these were. At first he had missed these similar themed markings on Samantha Turner. It had been an oversight due to the grief that had consumed him. In fact, he was well versed in the deeper meaning behind them, thanks, in no small part, to Doctor Winehouse. These were the signs of those involved in the cult called the **Illuminati**.

He remembered fragments of the many conversations he'd had with the Professor regarding the subject…

"The Illuminati is malevolent, Ethan; their plan is to change the world and rule as *dictators*! They consist of *13* bloodlines calling themselves 'The Black Nobility'. They have close ties to the *Vatican's* Black Pope. Manipulation and immense wealth *is* their power; they are consumed by it! They believe the key to total domination lies in the *occult*."

The next conversation was in a University classroom. Winehouse was speaking to him again. He had sounded so much more like a preacher than a scientist. So great, was his passion that he seemed obsessed with this...Illuminati.

"They are motivated by their hatred of God & humanity; portraying it as 'progress and freedom'. They are worshippers of Lucifer, the devil, who goes by many names: Satan, Baal, Seth, Samael. You must have faith in *yourself* or be lost forever in the embrace of hell, from which there is *no* escape!"

"Professor; are you saying that this organization has followers in the *government*," Ethan remembered asking.

 "Most of our world leaders, even today, are brought into power and chosen by their ability to lie and follow orders from the Illuminati! Open your eyes, Ethan, it has begun ages ago. This is *not* fiction! There is a *secret* war being fought; a war between *good and evil.* "

At one time, Ethan had thought that his fervent ramblings about the Illuminati were nothing more than fairytales. At the very least he had hoped that they were some crazy conspiracies held by a dear friend who had reached the vestiges of senility. *Today, that fairytale had become a very **real** nightmare.*

"Professor…"

"Listen to me! History is littered with the stench of the Illuminati. Hitler, Pol Pot, Stalin; they are but puppets of the so called 'New World Order'. The Illuminati will brand upon us the number of the beast, which is '666'. Those who accept it will most certainly be *destroyed.*"

His memories faded, as Ethan composed himself. There was something he was missing.

"Samael…of course; I should have remembered that," Ethan said out loud, "…but why *me*?"

There were things now that had clarity and reasons enough to find the truth. This was not only about finding Professor Winehouse's true killer anymore, but this cult has seen fit to bring out about his own demise. But why him; he was just a kid; a nobody.

He couldn't call the cops. Not anymore. If the Illuminati could so easily infiltrate the Boston P.D. who knew how many others were among them? The Professor and his father were gone. He had no one to turn to.

If he ran, he would obviously be wanted for the murder of a man who was one of their own. It was **his life** that was in danger; the police would probably not even believe him. After all, this was the 2nd murder scene he was present at. He needed to find the best course of action.

He looked down at the detective's revolver. It may be of some use, he thought to himself, and reached to pick it up. In the final moment, he decided against it. Ethan despised guns. He definitely knew how to handle one; his father, Earl Swan had taught him long ago. In his mind, however, guns were for the weak. It had always been a weapon for weak-minded fools, who tried to use it as a source of power against others. Anyone could shoot someone. Besides, he reflected to himself, he was much better with his fists.

Ethan rifled through the dead man's jacket and grabbed the small notebook. In the other pocket, he found a small device. It looked like a flash drive, but was slightly larger with tiny slots underneath. He put both of them into a compartment underneath his office desk. When he had a clear head, he would take a look at all of this. Now what to do about the dead guy?

The stone dead detective was close to 250 lbs. and rigor mortis had already started to set in. The stench of death was evident in the air.

Ethan kneeled down and began to wrap the body up into the rug and suddenly stopped. He shook and cleared his head. He almost laughed out loud at what he was about to do. He'd seen way too many movies.

"Jesus; that's just too *cliché*," he mumbled to himself, "What am I doing…"

He sat on the floor for a few moments and then pulled out his cell phone and called 911. He had no choice. If the cops were part of this, they'd get to him eventually anyway.

"Boston 911; what's the address of your emergency?"

"There's been a suicide….."

CHAPTER II - INSIGHT

BOSTON POLICE DEPARTMENT –

Ethan was brought into the bland, grey room and pushed roughly into a chair. The officer un-cuffed his hands and moved to stand by the door behind him. Ethan massaged his hands; the bastards had put the cuffs on him so tight, he felt like he was losing circulation. Looking down at his hands, he noticed that the redness cleared up immediately. The pain disappeared as well. He looked around at the room and waited for the obligatory 'good cop' and 'bad cop' to come in.

The room consisted of a small table and three chairs. A large tinted window built into the wall faced him; the only other source of color in the room. A recorder was placed on the table amongst a clutter of office supplies.

The door opened and two men entered the room. One was a heavy-set man in a black suit; his white shirt underneath, showing tiny red stains. The man breathed heavily as if consistently short of breath. The smaller of the two men simply wore a suit jacket and blue jeans. His gait and confidence in his walk seemed to make him the one in charge. He was athletically built and he could see the muscles straining against his shirt.

"My name is Detective Mahone, this is Detective Donnelly," He said, pointing to the larger man, "We have a lot of questions for you, son."

Ethan rolled his eyes. This *was* just like the movies.

"I've already given one of you my statement."

"I understand that kid, but a face to face is required. None of this makes any sense."

Ethan remained silent.

"You said that you hadn't seen Professor Winehouse in a few weeks, is that correct?"

The question took Ethan off guard.

"What has this got to do with Winehouse?"

"You described this…Detective Samael as being the one who showed up at Winehouse's murder scene. There must be a connection here."

"I have no idea who that guy is; he told me he was a cop! *Why do you think* I let him in?"

Mahone was visibly irritated. He smoothed his hands down his suit jacket.

"What I am trying to understand, Mr. Swan, is why a policeman or anybody else would want to kill *you*?"

"You know, Detective, when you find *that* out, *please* fill me in."

Ethan looked at the other detective. He was frantically scribbling away on a small notepad. He must be in a hurry to get back to the doughnuts, Ethan thought dryly to himself.

Mahone continued, "According to the background report, you are a very wealthy young man. You have a large trust fund in your name. It was awarded to you a few years ago by a Christopher Natash."

"It's *Chrisopth Natash*, the 'h' is silent," Ethan corrected, "You think they are after my *money*?"

Donnelly stopped writing and looked up at Ethan, then at Mahone.

"Holy shit, this guy's related to *Christoph Natash*?!"

"Where have I heard that name before," Mahone asked to himself.

"Where have you been, Mahone, everyone knows who Christoph Natash is! He's that billionaire whose son was murdered some years ago. It was the top story all over the news. Taylor Natash was his name; I helped on that case."

Ethan piped up. "I'm not really related to him; he's my Godfather. He is a very close family friend."

Mahone looked up seeming to remember something.

"He's a scientist, right? He owns that big fucking building: The Taylor Foundation. They helped finalize that Human Gene thing."

"It's called the Human Genome Project, and yes, he's a geneticist," Ethan replied.

"Do you think the perp was using the kid here to get to Natash," Donnelly interrupted.

Mahone looked back to Ethan inquisitively. He rubbed at his temples as he thought it over.

"You said this Samael showed you a *badge*?"

"Actually no; I recognized him from the crime scene. Why?"

Mahone seemed uncomfortable. He paused for a minute and took a deep breath.

"Kid, this guy is *not* one of us. We have no record of him. In fact, we've run his name and mug shot through the entire state and federal database. There is no law enforcement officer by the name of Samael – anywhere! The stranger thing is that the fingerprint analysis pulled up nothing; it's as if this guy does not even exist!"

Ethan looked visibly shaken. Donnelly pulled his chair closer to Ethan and handed him a card.

"Here's my card kid; what do you want to do? We can offer you protection if you want it. I would highly suggest you take us up on the offer."

"I'll keep your card," Ethan said, "but I can handle myself."

"I have no doubt of that Mr. Swan. As far as this case goes, we *will* be in touch.

Ethan was given the usual warnings, verbal threats and told not to go too far. Fortunately for

him, there was no concrete evidence to hold
him. He had done nothing, except defend
himself and the detectives seemed to be on his
side.

He was driven back to his condo and dropped
off at the entrance. He grudgingly took the
elevator back up to the 3rd floor and opened the
door to his condo. As he walked back inside, he
saw the blood-spattered remains and cleaned up
what he could and straightened up the living
room. Exhausted from everything, he fell down
into his bed headfirst and slept. Amazingly, he
was too tired to even think about his
misfortunes or his good friend's death.

Ethan woke up mid-evening to the sound of his
cell phone ringing. He answered to the accusing
sound of his Godfather's voice.

"It's about time you pick up; I've been trying to
call you for hours! What the hell is going on?!
Chief Stroh called me earlier this morning. He
said *my* godson may have been involved in two
murders!"

Christoph Natash's voice was comforting to
hear. He had always been there for Ethan
through thick and thin. Throughout his life,

Ethan had spent a great deal of time at his godfather's estate. There was always something to do there when his father was away. Ethan had always referred to him as 'Uncle', even though there were no true blood ties between them.

Natash was a very close family friend and Ethan's father had decreed him as godfather to his only son. He was a scientist of German decent and had came to this country in the 70's as a young man to make his considerable fortune; the American dream, so to speak.

Christoph was now in his late 60's, owned 2 international corporations, and a billionaire in his own right. Ethan remembered how he used to constantly remind him that his last name had a silent 'h'; pronounced 'Naa tas', not 'Natash'.

His domestic company, The Taylor Foundation had done some revolutionary work in the field of human genetics and was world renowned for their accomplishments. He also owned another company in Europe which had helped immensely in decoding the Human Genome Project. The Taylor Foundation was named after Christoph's first child, Taylor Natash.

Taylor had died at the tender age of six. The boy had been kidnapped and then brutally murdered. There had been no ransom demand; no phone calls; no evidence whatsoever. Taylor's body was found months later, washed up on Brighton Shore. His small frame was riddled with wounds; as if he had been stabbed repeatedly. Christoph had been too late to save him; but he had resolved to use all his resources and power to find out who had been responsible.

A year later, a middle-aged couple had been found; killed on the same shore. The investigation found that the couple had been involved in a child prostitution ring. Taylor's watch that Christoph had given to him on his 5th birthday had been found in their home.

For all practical purposes, Ethan always had a suspicion that Christoph had somehow avenged his son's murder. Christoph had never been the same since. He had become uptight and cautious; always eyeing others up with suspicion. It wasn't until the last few years, that Christoph had made peace with his son's death and returned to his jovial old self.

information was everywhere: the internet, books, and movies; most people had some idea of at least a shadow government existing within our own. He was indeed wealthy; did they want money? That didn't make sense. Everything he knew about the Illuminati made it very clear that their higher echelons had *more* than enough money. He was cocky, but he couldn't have pissed anyone off that badly.

Thinking about all of this, reminded him of the package he had been given by Cassie. Things had been happening so fast that he hadn't had much time to even open it, much less think about it. He had shoved the package under his Beansac when he had come into the condo. Why did he do *that*? It had been simple instinct, but most people would have just placed in on their coffee table.

He reached for the package, noticing that the plain brown paper wrapping had a Swathmore University logo on it. He did not see a return address of any kind on the packaging. He ripped it open. It was a hardcover book: H.G. Wells' The Open Conspiracy.

Ethan remembered this book; Professor Winehouse had given him a copy when they had first met years ago. The book was about embracing and promoting the 'New World Order'; Winehouse had told him it was important for Ethan to understand the other side and about their beliefs and goals. The thing was, the Professor already knew he had a copy. Why send him another? He studied the book for a minute then flipped through the pages. There was nothing unusual about it.

It was approaching 8 o'clock and his Uncle's mansion was close to a 45 minute drive. He jumped in the shower, got dressed, and packed some belongings. He put the book and his laptop into his backpack, grabbed his keys and went out the door. He really didn't want to stay at the condo too long anyway; no telling what else may happen. Getting into his car, he felt refreshed.

Roxbury, MA was a rough area; similar to lower Harlem. Riots, rampant arson, and violent crime had been a part of the town's history for centuries. It was noted for its hilly geography and in the 1600's, the early settlers had established a series of villages and the First Church of Roxbury, which served as not only a place of worship, but a meeting place for government.

 He had always wondered *why* Christoph had chosen to live in that neighborhood. He could buy any piece of property he wanted, yet he had built a mansion on the outskirts of *this* town.

Driving on the open highway, Ethan felt alone. It wasn't that there were hardly any cars on the road; it was more emotional than anything else. He had been a vibrant child growing up; making lots of friends, throwing parties, and dating many beautiful women. He was still confident and secure, but since his father had died, he had kept people at an arm's distance. He had lost many friends in the grievance process he had gone through. He had turned people away; not returned their calls; ignored their help. Even Jennna Reinholdt, his long-time girlfriend had given up on him and gone her own way.

Now, heading to Christoph's house, he felt like he had a second chance to put his past behind him; at least for some time. Christoph had always understood him; especially his complicated feelings about his father.

Ethan pulled into the long driveway leading to Natash's enormous estate. The once, lush green grass of the lawn was now slowly dying. At the center, there was a beautiful fountain which sprang an angelic figure; her arms outstretched towards the lower waterspout waiting for something to appear.

Four marble columns of white & black arose from the foundation like great factory smokestacks. Two large gargoyle statues made of the blackest of ebony were perched on either side of the main doorway, as if they were ready to pounce on their unsuspecting prey. He pushed the button on the intercom and a harsh voice came forth.

"Can I help you?"

"I'm here to see my Uncle Christoph. "

"Of course Mr. Swan, please do come in."

As he opened the door, a large well-dressed man came to greet him. Uncle Christoph must have hired a new butler. The man reminded him of a haughty 'nose in the air' Englishman. If it were not for the bland black dress of his service profession, he could pass for a thug bouncing at any nightclub in Boston.

"Right this way Sir."

The interior was as beautiful as he had remembered. The looming vaulted ceilings reminded Ethan of the inside of John the Baptist, a Church he used to frequent after his father died. The various crystal vases and sculptures scattered the hallway.

The man led him into the spacious living room where he was then greeted by his godfather, Christoph Natash. Natash was a tall man, around 6 feet 2 with a beak for a nose and peppered grey hair. He dressed splendidly, this time in a dark black suit with a red tie for contrast. He was very distinguished and pleasant as always.

"How are you son, so good to see you! It's been some time since you were here last!" Christoph embraced him in a warm hug.

Ethan didn't reply. He was taken aback with the young lady seated on the couch.

"I assume you remember Angelica," said Christoph, noticing Ethan's wandering eyes.

The gorgeous young woman with flowing black hair jumped from her seat and rushed towards Ethan, taking him into a huge embrace.

"Ethan! You look great; how are you?! It's been so long."

Ethan hugged her back and smiled. He hadn't seen Angelica for almost 9 years. She was Christoph's daughter. They used to play together as kids and were best of friends in those days. She was his first crush.

Angelica had left home to start a new life in Santa Monica, California. There, she had enlisted in the marines and had then gone on to become a high paid model three years ago. At least, that was what he had heard through the grapevine. He took a long, hard look at her. God, she was beautiful; definitely filled out in all the right places. She carried herself with confidence and stature like she always had.

"Ange....I didn't even recognize you! You're looking good. Where've you been?"

That was an understatement for the woman in front of him. Her long, black hair swept down from her exquisite face and sharply contrasted her deep hazel eyes. Long, slender legs came down from beneath her tight leather skirt; the clothes framing her like an exquisite work of art.

"I'm sure you've heard. The military was just not for me; I'm still modeling for Fraction Magazine," she said, and then hesitated, "Forget about me. I heard what happened to *you*. Are you okay?"

"Yes. Why don't you tell us exactly *what* is going on," interrupted Christoph as he offered him a glass of wine.

Ethan sat down on one of the leather couches, put his pack down and took a deep breath. He explained as best he could what had transpired during the last two days. He intentionally left out the details of the package and what he had taken off the two killers. He didn't quite know why, but he had always trusted his instincts. The less they knew; the safer they'd be. Regardless, he remembered, some of those things were still at his place.

Four glasses of wine later, he finished his tale to the combined astonishment of everyone present.

"Oh my God," exclaimed Angelica, "What are you going to do now?!"

"I don't have much of a choice. I have to find out *what* is happening here. My life's been turned upside down and the only way I see to get out of this mess alive, is to find the answers," replied Ethan.

"Let's just all calm down for a minute," said Christoph, "You're in some serious trouble here. Have you seen the paper, Ethan?"

"No," Ethan replied, "Why?"

Christoph slid him the local newspaper. There was an article about him on the front page.

'**BOSTON, MA** – What appeared to be the attempted murder of Ethan Swan, a young student at Swathmore University have police baffled. Swan says he was approached for questioning by a detective from the Boston police department at his condo in Breck Bay. The Boston P.D. however states that the man does not exist. The detective….'

Ethan stopped reading; he didn't have to go any further. He pushed the newspaper away.

"They know where I live; they know I'm still alive."

Natash nodded in agreement.

"Let me speak with Chief Stroh tomorrow; there *has* to be something he can do," Christoph replied, "It's late. Angelica will show you to your room. Try to get some sleep."

Sleep? Sleep was the furthest thing on his mind right now. They knew where he lived and worked! He would be stuck here until this was over, if it ever was. What now? Angelica stood up and took Ethan's arm in hers.

"It'll be okay Ethan. My father will be able to help. Come on."

Ethan grabbed his pack and went with Angelica. He paused and turned towards Natash.

"Thank you Uncle Christoph; I appreciate this."

The billionaire nodded in reply.

Angelica brought Ethan to a spacious room on the far side of the hall. It was decorated with bold ornamentation and had pictures hanging on the walls with contrasting red and black elements. Heavy moldings aligned the walls and two large twisted columns rose up from the floor. Baroque architecture, Ethan remembered, had influenced Western Europe in the 17th Century.

"I'll see you in the morning, okay?"

Ethan smiled back at her in response. He started unloading his pack.

"And Ethan..."

"Yeah..?"

"It's really good to see you again," said Angelica as she left the room and closed the door.

He pulled out the remaining clothes and hung them in the closet; he placed his laptop on the office desk in the corner and powered it on. He just couldn't sleep right now. The last thing he pulled out was the book that had been mailed to him from Professor Winehouse.

There *has* to be something here, he thought to himself. Page after page, he analyzed to no avail. Nothing was unusual about it. He reached down to put the book down and noticed that the back cover was larger than the front. He opened the book to the bottom cover and peered at it for a moment. He firmly brought his hand across the middle.

There was something in it. It was sewn completely around; perfectly. Ethan grabbed a silver letter opener off the desk and dug carefully into the stitching.

He tore it open and saw it contained a recordable DVD. He turned it over in his hands. It was blank; no writing or notation of any kind. This was obviously what Winehouse had hoped he would find. He logged in and put the disk in the DVD drive. The clear image of Professor Winehouse peered back at him from the screen.

"When I was a child, my Sunday school teacher filled me in on much of what was to come. Yes, even then we had a fair understanding of the Illuminati. I am not here to preach; only to help you understand; to open your eyes, if you will. Many of their secrets are well guarded, but this is what we do know."

"Their objective has always been one thing: world domination. To accomplish this, they must unite the world under one person or group dedicated to the Illuminati's twisted ambitions. This will *require* 3 things: a one-world government, a one-world religion, and a one-world currency. These changes have been subtle at best; if brought on in full force, the people of the world would realize what was to come. Have you not noticed the delicate changes to monetary currency; from new quarters to magnetic strips in bills?"

"The ultimate goal is the introduction of a 'Smart Card'. This card will be embedded into the wrist of every human being, with the last 3 digits ending in 666, the Mark of the Beast. It will contain each individual's entire background including their social security number, banking information, medical history; everything the conspiratorial hierarchy will need for one thing: Control. Privacy will be non-existent. The Holy Bible states that those who accept the Mark, will be damned to burn in hell for all eternity!"

"The dollar bill itself has been embedded with the Illuminati's symbols and secret code since its conception. The pyramid on the face is a pagan temple of Satan Worship; 'Novus Ordo Seclorum' translates to the 'New World Order'; the eye of Horus, called the all-seeing eye, above the pyramid represents the eye of Lucifer; the number thirteen layered into many of the images in the bill is a significant number of ill-omen."

Even though he knew about the Illuminati as a cult, some of these revelations were a surprise to him. A light knock came at the door. Instinctively, Ethan quickly ejected the disk and placed it back into the book's binding.

"Just a minute," he said to the unseen person.

"Ethan, it's Angelica," she replied back.

Ethan put the book carefully back in his pack and opened the door. He'd have to come back to the disk later. What was Angelica doing here at this hour?

Angelica was stunning as usual. She was clad in a rather flimsy nightgown that accentuated her curvaceous figure. Her long legs were visible right below her thighs. She came in and hugged him.

"Hey you, I can't sleep. I saw your light on"

"Yeah, I'm just catching up on some research;" replied Ethan, "take a seat."

They both sprawled out across the enormous bed. She looked into his eyes as if she wanted to tell him something important.

"How've you been?" asked Ethan.

"Well…I'm home for good now. My father is ecstatic about it; he never wanted me to leave home in the first place. He always tells me that there is nothing more important than blood; you know how he is. I'm actually relieved I'm back too."

"It's good to see you, Ange," Ethan said, "I've been so busy; otherwise I would have called to catch up."

"It's okay," she laughed, "You don't have to make any excuses for *ignoring* me all those *years*!"

"No…I…That's not what…"

"Ethan!"

"What?"

"Shut up already; really, it's okay; I just missed you is all."

Ethan laughed.

"I haven't seen you for *so long*, Ange," he said, "You used to be such a tomboy! What happened to you?"

"Living in California can work *wonders* on a gal; besides I had to get a date *somehow*! The tomboy look just didn't do too well for the guys."

Ethan hadn't realized how much he'd missed her until he saw her again. They had always gotten along so well; he had always wondered why he hadn't made a move on her. Seeing her before him, he felt like kicking himself in the ass.

"Ethan; I'm so sorry to hear about your Professor. Father told me he was very close to you. If there is anything I could do…"

"Ange," he interrupted, "I don't really want to talk about it, okay?"

"Okay," she replied, nervously pulling her hand through her hair, "I'm sorry."

They were silent for a few moments. Ethan moved closer to her.

"I heard about your stint as G.I. Jane some years ago. I never figured you for the military, Ange."

Angelica's voice seemed strained as she began to speak.

"Yeah…well…"

P a g e

Angelica turned her head to the side.

"Ange; are you okay?"

She hesitated for a moment, and then looked him dead in the eyes.

"Ethan....we...I...did some things. We...were ordered to. I shouldn't talk about it; its classified information...but I *need* to tell someone...I know the last thing you need right now is to deal with *my* problems, but..."

"I understand how you feel, Ange; believe me I do. Please...it's okay."

Angelica had a frightened, yet serious look on her face. She shifted her body up into an upright position.

"I'm listening, go on," Ethan prodded.

"I'm sure you've heard of Nabuhn; it was a thriving village on the outskirts of the Congo."

"I have. I read the article in World News; more than 10,000 people were slaughtered by the Rathnok Militia. It disgusted me that human beings are capable of that sort of thing."

"I know, the people of Nabuhn were highly civilized. They had been taught English twenty years back by American Missionaries. They even developed a fundamental Christian religion and were in the process of becoming an independently governed nation."

Angelica was visibly shaking now. Ethan gently touched her arm as a sign of reassurance.

"What *happened,* Ange? Where are you going with this?"

Angelica looked away; her eyes lost in thought.

"It was a joint mission with the CIA; not usual for a Marine Platoon," Angelica stated, "We were sent there to prevent an airborne viral outbreak from spreading. It was called the Dola Virus. We were told it would be an epidemic. It was incurable; no vaccine or treatment of any kind. Those that had been infected were deemed already dead!"

"Dola Virus? That doesn't ring a bell; what is it?" inquired Ethan.

"From what we were briefed, it is a mutated strain of Ebola. It destroys your body from inside out! It starts with an infection inside your red blood cells which spreads through the central nervous system, bringing your body into a coma-like sleep until you simply don't wake up. Symptoms were a very high white blood cell count, lesions on the body, and chronic fatigue."

Angelica turned back and locked eyes with Ethan.

"They sent the troops into that village and they killed every man, woman, and child to keep the world and humanity, safe from the Virus. The soldiers were told that it was for the greater good; to save mankind from a devastating disease."

Angelica broke down, tears flooding her eyes. He body wracked with sobs as Ethan held her tightly.

"Ange…..I don't know what to say. I'm…I'm sorry you had to go through that."

Angelica looked back and up into his face. She slowly calmed down and pulled herself together.

"Ethan…you don't understand! The Rathnok Militia had been disbanded months before! It was us; my platoon…*we* killed those people and the murders were blamed on the Militia!"

"What," Ethan exclaimed in shock.

"I….knew a man there; he was killed a year after the incident at Nabuhn. We were…close. He was a doctor with the CDC. He was prevented by the military from doing any autopsy of the bodies."

Angelica held Ethan tighter.

"He tried to approach the top Brass about it; that was the last I heard from him! Don't you see? It was *intentional*; someone *wanted* those people dead!"

As he held Angelica, Ethan could feel the anger well up inside him. He had never trusted the government or the military, but the cold awareness that they could sink to this level upset him considerably. The murders of thousands of innocents weighed heavily on his mind. Angelica, he noticed had drifted off into a much warranted sleep. He felt his own eyelids getting heavy.

His dreams did *not* come easy. Flashes of images and light flooded his brain. It was like an old movie reel. He caught glimpses of wars being fought; Nazi's executing innocent Jews, a black mass, and then priests wearing black cowls in discussion around a large red table with a black pentagram in the middle. Their reptilian eyes bored into his soul as if he was sitting directly in front of them. The images blurred into what seemed like businessmen having an important meeting. Their clothing had changed, but they had the same eyes. The scene went red, and then promptly black as night.

Ethan woke up to a cold sweat. He glanced at the clock; it was close to 1 o'clock in the afternoon. Angelica was no longer in his arms. She must be awake by now. He jumped in the shower, got dressed, and left his room. Walking into the kitchen, Angelica saw him and smiled. She slid him a cup of tea.

"I didn't want to wake you; you looked like you needed the sleep. Thanks for last night."

"Anytime Ange, I hope it helped," Ethan said as he stirred three heaping spoons of sugar into his caffeinated drink. He was really hungry. He grabbed a donut from the table and finished it quickly. "I just hope Christoph is not angry with me. He wanted to see if Chief Stroh could be of any help."

"Ethan, my father was called away on another one of his *urgent* business trips. He asked me to tell you that he is very sorry but he would speak with you once he gets back, in a few days."

What?! Deep down he felt resentment towards Christoph. Why had he left without saying anything? This was *his life* that was in danger! It had better have been far more urgent than his own predicament. Even such, the old man *had* taken him in...

"That's fine Ange; I understand his obligations. I feel better being here anyway."

"He's a busy man; he really wants to help. It's just that running all these companies keeps him away a lot. He thinks of you as a son, you know. Since Taylor died..."

Angelica looked as if she was going to break down and cry right there in the kitchen.

"We'll figure this out when he has time; it's okay. Let's get out of here; it'll do us *both* some good!"

Angelica remained silent in thought for another moment.

"Father said we could take the horses down Midland Trail today; maybe we can get our minds off all this and have some fun for a change. I'm going to run up and get changed, okay? We'll have to take your car."

Ethan looked up from his steaming cup.

"You know, that actually sounds like a good plan. I'm in."

Ethan watched her walk upstairs and sighed. She was a *stunning* woman, he thought to himself. Taking the horses out seemed like a *great* idea. Angelica and he would ride all the time when they were younger. Besides, with these frequent nightmares he'd been having, maybe a new scene would help.

He quickly ate two more donuts and got up from the table. He went to his room and grabbed his jacket and car keys. He was excited at the prospect of spending more time with Angelica. Perhaps he could sort things through on his own if he had a clear head.

Ethan met Angelica at the front alcove. She was dressed in riding gear and carried two helmets in her left hand. She looked cute and ridiculous all at the same time.

"Well, aren't you the *professional* equestrian," Ethan said, jokingly.

"Fuck off," she said, motioning to the riding helmets, "Are you ready?"

"I sure am," Ethan replied, dangling the keys in front of her.

They loaded the gear into Ethan's BMW and got situated in the car. He wondered to himself if it was a good idea taking a sports car into the wooded trails.

The ranch leading to Midland Trail was close to an hour away from the mansion. Christoph used it to entertain his VIP clients and of course, for his own recreation. It was located in a secluded wooded area, complete with numerous trails for horse-back riding and hiking.

The weather was overcast, but there was no forecast for rain. He put the car into drive and followed the driveway down to the road.

Ethan turned the news radio station on to catch up on anything he might have missed the last few days. He always liked to stay up to date on current events.

The newscaster's voice was solemn as he was finishing a top story.

"....derailed today, killing 400 people. The train had left from Hoboken, New Jersey and was heading towards Middleton, New York. The entire commuter system is in disarray; rioting has ensued with family and friends of the victims passing blame on the transit system's safety regulations."

Ethan quickly switched the station. The next announcement was also grim.

"....and peace talks have quickly evaporated. Hans Aleksander, the National Security Advisor says that war is inevitable."

This was ridiculous. He turned the radio to a music station.

"Sorry," he said sheepishly to Angelica.

"It's okay. I always hated the news. It's *depressing*," she said in response.

Ethan felt comfortable around Angelica. He felt he could trust her. Maybe he should confide in her about what he had found. After all, he did not have anyone else to turn to. He turned onto the country road that headed towards the ranch.

"Ange…I'd like to tell you something. I've been hesitant to share some personal information; I'm sorry I didn't tell you before."

"With your recent turn of events, I don't blame you," she laughed.

"I just didn't want to get you and your father involved. I don't know what I'd do if anything ever happened to you."

"Ethan, we're *already* involved. I may not be a detective, but the Taylor Foundation *does* have its resources."

With that, he proceeded to tell her of the items he had found on the cultists, the disk that he had received from Professor Winehouse, and the recent nightmares he had been having.

Pulling the car into the ranch, he was relieved. He had held all of it inside for quite some time now. Angelica had absorbed it all in, not judging him one way or the other. He felt that they now shared a unique bond and was sure that he could trust her. He turned to Angelique looking at him with inquisitive eyes.

"It felt like he was trying to warn me of something. I was only partway through when you came in."

"Maybe he was. With everything that's happened and his murder, I'd bet he was onto something," replied Angelica, "Would you mind if I took a look?"

"When we get back, that's the first thing we'll do. You may see something I don't."

"The *nightmares* are something else. What about this flash drive?"

"They're back at my condo. I didn't trust the P.D.; in fact, I don't know *who* to trust!"

You can trust *me*, she thought. She stared at him in concern for a few seconds. With everything he'd been through, she was amazed he had been keeping it together so well.

"We'll figure it out Ethan," she said, lightly touching his arm, "together."

CHAPTER III – SECT

They came to the ranch and pulled into the parking stall. While unpacking their gear, they noticed that there was an old beat up truck already there.

The approximately 40 acres of the ranch which lay out before them was an impressive sight to behold. White vinyl pasture fencing encircled the exterior of the ranch. A large barn with four covered stalls and attached outdoor runs loomed in the distance. There was a full sized riding arena off to the side. Views of the surrounding valley and the natural trails perfectly contrasted with the rest of the dark brown ranch.

The caretaker came out to meet them. His name was William Hicks and Ethan remembered him from long ago when they used to come here as kids. He was an elderly gentleman about in his mid 60's now. Hicks had been with Christoph for quite a long time; he had been entrusted with the duties of the ranch. He lived just down the road in a small home with just his wife as company.

His thin frame did not belie the fact that he was a hard worker. He carried himself upright and confident as he walked towards them. The old man was as sharp as a razor and his wrinkled eyes instantly lit up with recognition as the two stepped out of the car.

"Ethan! Angelica! Come here and give me a hug; it's been a *long* time! I sure didn't expect to see you two here."

"Hey Will," replied Ethan as he put his arms around Hicks, "How you doing? I thought you'd be six feet under by now!"

"I can still kick *your* young ass! You'd be amazed what this Viagra can do!"

"Hi Will," said Angelica as she embraced him tightly.

"Angelica; you still hanging around with this *young buck*," said the old man, sarcastically.

"Yeah…well, we can't always choose the people who we associate with," answered Angelica.

Will laughed.

"I thought you two were more of Christoph's bland executives; they come here now and then.

I was just on my way out, but I think you kids can handle things from here."

"Aww, come on Will, stay a while," said Ethan.

"No can do amigo, I promised the wife I'd be home; it's our anniversary tonight. You know how it goes. I'll come back to visit with you two in the morning. I'll bring the horses out before I go though."

"Alright Will," Angelica piped in, "but promise me you'll be back tomorrow, okay?"

"Will do sweetheart, you take care now."

Will Hicks grabbed his things, brought the horses out, and got into his truck. Ethan and Angelica waved goodbye to the old man as he drove off.

They tied up the horses and were about to go indoors when Ethan noticed something out of the corner of his eye. A dark figure was watching them from the woods by an outcrop of trees. Ethan dropped the lead and instinctively sprinted towards the forest.

"Ethan...what the...wait..." Angelica called out in vain.

Ethan ignored her and ran for the shadow waiting in the trees. As he got closer, he saw that the man had a knife strapped to his waist. He went into a crouch, and then brought his elbow right into the man's side. The stranger lost his breath as Ethan grabbed him by the throat, holding his arm away from the knife with his other hand.

"Who *are* you," Ethan demanded in a threatening tone.

The man was visibly shaken and stammered back in a hoarse voice.

"Look…I don't….want any trouble fella," he said gasping for breath, "I'm just…on a hike…I'm sorry if….I scared ya."

Ethan eased up on his throat and relaxed his grip. He took a good look at the stranger in front of him. He *was* dressed in camouflage pants and hiking boots; he had greasy black hair falling over his face and a cleft lip. Beady little eyes peered at Ethan from under his full brim hat.

There was a partially covered tattoo that could be seen through his half-buttoned shirt: it looked like the letters spelled 'OI'.

The man took a deep breath for some much needed air. He stared at them angrily.

"The name's Red Haskins. I live not too far from here and I take this hike every damned day. Just what the hell is *wrong* with you boy?"

Ethan let him go and looked up at Red.

"I'm sorry… Sir, I saw you watching us and….."

"I was looking at those fine animals you got there; *not* you two. I fancy myself a bit of a horse lover. You got a problem with that?"

"I…Errr…"

Ethan felt stupid; paranoid at the very least.

"I'll be off now if *you will*."

"Sir…please," began Angelica, overhearing the conversation. She had caught up to them.

Red abruptly cut her off with a wave of his hand and disappeared back into the woods.

Angelica hit Ethan on the arm as he stupidly stared ahead. He could tell that she was irritated with him.

"What the *hell* was that," she exclaimed.

"Sorry," replied Ethan, "With everything that's happened the last few days, I thought…"

"He *was* a bit odd," Angelica said soothingly, "Just forget about him. Let's get on the trails; the weather is looking a bit gloomy."

"Sorry," Ethan insisted again and turned around back towards the horses.

They un-tethered the horses and adjusted the saddles. Horus and Armen Ra were hot-blooded Arabian horses; Horus was chestnut in color, Armen Ra, being black as night. They were both good-natured and very intelligent animals. Horus took to Ethan almost immediately even though he was a complete stranger to him. What stupid names, Ethan thought as he sat firmly in the saddle.

"My father named them after Egyptian gods; can you *believe* that," said Angelica as if reading his mind.

"*Interesting* names," he replied. He didn't realize Chritoph had such a fascination with Egyptian mythology.

"Let's take the East entrance," said Angelica, "it curves back through the Midland Trail."

Together, they entered the awaiting woods. Ethan remembered this path from when he was younger. It bent in crooked angles through the woods, then winded down past a natural waterfall, and finally ran into the Midland Trail. The Trail had been there since the 1600's and was virtually untouched by the outside world.

All the way around and back to the ranch was close to 30 miles in total distance. He didn't know why Angelica liked this Trail so much; after all, you couldn't take the horses at full gallop until you entered the Midland. The most they could do was a slow gait and he liked to go *fast*.

"You know; you seemed to like doing this much more when we were kids," she laughed.

"Well, you know how we *old timers* are," Ethan retorted back with a grin.

They enjoyed each other's company, remembering old times and cracking jokes every so often. As they neared the waterfall, Angelica stopped Armen Ra gently with her stirrups and got down.

"I *love* this place; come on you Ass, get down here!"

Ethan laughed, leaped out of the saddle and grabbed the blanket that was wrapped neatly to the side. Angelica was halfway down the small side trail heading towards a large, looming rock by the waterfall.

She was sitting on its rough, flat surface and skipping stones by the time he caught up. He sat down next to her and laid the colorful blanket upon the rocks. He reached down and scooped some stones of his own.

They sat silently, skipping rocks in the water. It had been ages since they had been here. The bare trees and the sound of the waterfall were quite peaceful to him.

Angelica smiled at him, cupped her hand under his chin and kissed him deeply.

Ethan pulled back after a minute and looked at her in shock. What was she doing and why did it feel so natural.

"Don't look so *surprised*. You *know* you wanted that," she said with a big grin.

"Your right, I did. What *took* you so long," Ethan laughed.

"Oh, shut up and kiss me."

His tongue caught hers as they intertwined; wet with passion. He cautiously moved his kisses from her lips to her neck; to her chest; over her breast; then down her stomach. She moaned in anticipation. He slowly brought his hand down; barely touching her inner thigh. She drew in a sharp breath as she felt his hand grasping her. Ethan had fantasized about this more than a few times since seeing her again, but his mind reeled in indecision.

His thoughts came sporadically. He and Angelica were best of friends. What if this ended badly? Would they lose what they'd had? Was he being selfish for getting her involved in all of this? Would she be hurt if she were with him?

Ethan suddenly stopped and pulled back from Angelica. He put his hand to his mouth and coughed.

"Ange; I…I can't have you involved with me; not now! This is a bad idea."

Angelica reeled back and stared at him angrily.

"*That* is *my* choice, Ethan. I'm well aware of the *danger* in your life right now. I care about you; I always have. Don't push me away!"

In the thick of the looming trees, the snapping of broken twigs could be heard. The unmistaken sound of footsteps disappeared as quickly as it had come.

Ethan looked towards the woods and held out his hand to Angelica. Something was wrong.

"Not now Ange, okay," he urged.

He helped her up as he peered into the trees.

"Ethan," Angelica began; only to be shushed by a hand to her lips.

Ethan walked over to the noise and inspected it further. Angelica was looking at him in confusion. Parting the branches, he didn't see anyone. There were no footprints or broken branches. Feeling relieved, he motioned for Angelica to come forward.

"Are you getting a little *paranoid* again," Angelica asked him.

"What are you; my psychiatrist," he answered sarcastically.

"Oh…shut up!"

They both laughed as they climbed back onto the horses. He still could not shake the strange feeling that something was amiss. Ethan turned back to her.

"I promise; we'll talk later, okay?"

Angelica nodded and turned her horse back towards the trail.

"Let's get going, it looks like a storm is blowing in," she said.

Ethan looked to the sky. Heavy clouds extended from east to west and the sky was slowly turning a grayish color. A flock of geese were flying overhead. They were definitely *signs* of a storm approaching. How do I know that, he thought to himself, as he turned his horse in stride behind Angelica.

They returned to the trail and brought their horses to a steady gallop, heading towards the intersection to Midland. The path opened up into a small clearing of low brush and grassland. A dilapidated cabin stood eerily against the trees to the East side. He'd been on this trail since they were kids and this is the first time he had seen this cabin.

Ethan thought he heard a weak scream amongst the wind whistling through the air. He glanced at Angelica; she was riding in step, oblivious to the sounds.

Ethan stopped his horse and pulled her back around. He got down from the saddle; Angelica followed suit.

"What are you doing," she asked, inquisitively.

"Did you hear that?"

"Hear what; what are you talking about," she questioned.

He tied the horse's reins onto a post alongside the front of the cabin.

"I don't remember this place being here before, *do you?*"

"Ethan, it *has* been close to ten years you know," she replied.

"Let's get the horses some water," he lied. He didn't really know why, but his instincts told him this was somehow important.

"Alright, hurry up then."

They approached the worn wooden door and knocked. There was a large decorative sign attached to the door. It was made of straw and resembled an upside down cross.

They knocked a few times; no answer came forth. There was no knob of any kind so Ethan put a little pressure on it and the door opened. It was dark and quiet; the only light was from the fading rays of sunshine coming through the open windows.

"We can't just walk in," protested Angelica, "someone obviously lives here."

"I know," replied Ethan as he stepped inside. Angelica followed without another word.

The large room stretched in front of them was disgusting. Small animal pens constructed of chicken wire were to the left side of the room. Half-eaten food, some of which looked like oversized turkey legs were sitting atop the oval table. Flies and roaches swarmed the leftover red congealed substance dripping off onto the ground.

There was a hole, cut out into the middle of the table that had curved sharp edges along the outside. It looked like a circular blade. The smell emanating from the stench of the place burned their nostrils. Up ahead, there was an opening that led down into a flight of stairs to a lower room; a basement of some kind.

"What the *hell* is that," exclaimed Angelica, pointing at the table, "It smells like rotting meat!"

"Shhhh."

Ethan could not make out the hushed whispers coming from the lower room below, but there was someone definitely down there. There it was again; a faint scream.

"Get outside *now*," he ordered Angelica.

"But, what are…."

"Just do it," he said abruptly.

After watching to make sure Angelica had gone outside, he slowly made his way down the steps. They opened up into another room that had a tunnel dug into the wall. He had to crouch down to make it in, but it was big enough for a man to walk through.

The tunnel was musty and bugs of all kinds were scurrying about. He hated bugs. Quietly coming out on the other side, he almost ran into what looked like giant wine barrels. They were spread about the large cavern like decorative items.

The voices were stronger now; his eyes focused themselves in the dim light of the room. He ducked behind one of the barrels and peered around to see what was taking place.

Two men were in the room. They had on masks, which appeared to be in the shape of a goat with horns and were stripped from the waist up. Ancient markings lined their upper torsos in occult designs. He could now make out a strange chanting emanating from their lips. They were seated, Indian style, their arms coming down with evident thrusts; blood flying off the glinting blades of their knives.

He stood up now, anger taking over his being and slowly crept closer. An unbidden rage swelled up in him that he had not known he was capable of.

A dead young woman lay before the two men in the middle of a large black pentagram; jagged holes lining her body, blood everywhere. The thick black candles burned tirelessly, casting shadows in an eerie way. It appeared to be some kind of black magic ritual; a ritual that involved human sacrifice!

The beat of Ethan's heart drowned out the chanting, as his anger swelled within his very soul. He had to do something!

Ethan ran up behind the larger of the two men, grabbed his head and twisted quickly. The man died instantly and collapsed to the floor. The other man stood up, peering back curiously at Ethan. He put his knife threateningly out before him, holding his ground. Ethan recognized the style of knife: it was a Khukuri blade.

Ethan let go of the dead man's neck and proceeded to walk towards the other man. He was furious and livid with anger at the senseless slaughter he had just witnessed.

"My God…what have you done?!"

The strange man tensed as he stood up and Ethan could somehow tell that he was staring directly into his eyes from behind the mask.

"*God*? God is not here, boy! The Dark Lord reigns *here* and you have *spoiled* the ritual!"

Ethan looked around him. There was nothing he could use as a weapon and this man had a blade the size of a small sword. He could feel his heartbeat banging at his chest, but surprisingly his head was clear and in focus. He knew just what to do as he took another step closer.

"I know who you are Ethan Swan," said the man flatly, "more so, I know *what* you are. Either way, you *will* die tonight!"

Ethan stopped dead in his tracks. Had he heard that right? How could this be?

"How do you know my name," he asked.

The man reached for his face and pulled off his mask, knife still outstretched in his hand. Greasy black hair fell over Red's face. He spoke differently than at their earlier encounter. He twirled the blade in his hand.

Ignoring the question, Red leaped for Ethan with the blade. Ethan dodged the swipe, parried to the side and sent a powerful punch to the side of Red's head, knocking him back.

"Ethan!"

Angelica had obviously decided to ignore his advice of staying put. He turned towards her voice just slightly. It was enough of a distraction for Red to close in on him again.

"Stay back," he yelled at her.

"You're pathetic," Red screamed, as he rushed towards Ethan, "I *see why*, you've been scheduled for execution!"

A throb of pain shot through him as Red sliced him in the forearm. It wasn't too deep, but it sure stung. That *wouldn't* happen again. He ducked to the side under the big man's next thrust, seized the knife hand with one arm and twisted, exposing Red's elbow. He slammed his other hand, palm first into the naked joint, breaking his elbow with a loud snap.

As the Khukuri fell from Red's grasp, Ethan went into a crouch and caught the handle as it fell with his right hand. He brought his right knee down and swung the blade in a sweeping arc across Red's thighs.

Deep gashes spread from corner to corner of both legs as blood spurted forth like a fountain.

Red screamed in pain as his legs collapsed in, throwing him to the ground. Using his free hand, Ethan balled it into a fist and struck the defeated man in the throat. The windpipe caved in as Red tried in vain to catch some precious breaths.

As Ethan watched, the big man stumbled to the ground and fell back against the wall, coming to a seated position. Choking on his blood and spittle, Red managed to turn his head towards Ethan and glared at him wickedly.

"You…are not…*one of us!*"

His remaining breaths were labored; his eyes rolled up into his head as he died.

His violent actions hit Ethan like a hammer to the stomach. He doubled over and threw up the contents of his stomach. This was the first time ever, that he had used his considerable skills to take a human life. He felt sick. He'd had no choice; they deserved it, didn't they? Whichever way he looked at it or whatever he told himself, he couldn't shed the feeling of disgust he had for himself just now.

"Ethan, are you alright," Angelica asked soothingly massaging his back.

Ethan didn't reply. He waved her off.

"It's not your fault," she prodded knowingly, "they tried to kill you; they murdered that poor girl."

Ethan looked up at her. She was visibly shaken, but held her ground. Her concern for him far outweighing the fear she now felt. She was a tough one. He wiped at his mouth and straightened himself up. He winced and knew that the cut on his arm was deeper than he thought.

"I'm okay," he finally replied as he walked up to Red's body.

"What did he mean, Ethan? He *knew* who you were! *How is that possible*; I've never even seen this man before today?"

He did not know what to tell her. There were no words to comfort either of them. What he had witnessed and what he had heard did not make any sense to him. They just led to more questions.

"I don't...know, Ange. I...don't know anything anymore..."

Ethan didn't look back at her as he bent down and searched Red's body that lay before him. He could now see the entire tattoo he had failed to comprehend before. They were not letters, as he had surmised; rather numerals.

-2-0-1-2-

"It wasn't 'O.I.'", he said to himself, "it's two thousand twelve; it's a year!"

"What are you talking about," Angelica inquired, "what do you mean it's a *year*?"

"It has to do with the ancient Mayan civilization. They were an advanced culture for their time and known for many accomplishments; their calendar system in particular. For some who practice the occult or Satanism, December 21st, 2012 is a day of great significance. The Earth will be in a period of cosmic alignment at that time. It is supposed to be the dawn of a new era or *maybe* even the beginning of *Armageddon*; the end of the world."

Angelica looked at him confusingly and let out a sigh. All the vibrant energy she once had was gone. She barely held herself up as she leaned against the bare rock.

"You don't really believe... all that superstition, do you? This is really happening to us; it's not some fantasy!"

Ethan locked eyes with her for a moment, but remained silent. He looked back down to the dead assassin.

As he searched Red's pockets, a small device dropped to the floor. It was a flash drive; unusual in size, like the one he had found on the detective. On it, a tiny sliver of metal was attached, but was chipped.

"I've seen one of these before," Ethan said to Angelica, showing her the device, "I found one just like it on the cultist who tried to kill *me* and on the woman who murdered Professor Winehouse."

"What is it," asked Angelica. She had composed herself quickly.

"It looks like a flash drive. My guess is this metal sliver with the markings holds the data; this one is obviously broken. We need to go."

"What about the woman?"

Ethan looked toward her bloody remains.

"We can't do anything for her now, Ange; we have to leave this place," he replied solemnly.

She was silent for a moment and then turned hysterically towards him.

"We need to call the police, Ethan! We need to get some help. We can't do this on our own anymore! Please!"

He considered it as his thoughts turned in various scenarios. Maybe she was right, but then again…

"How can we *trust* them, Ange? These…people seem to be everywhere! There have been more attempts on my life than I care to discuss. I don't know what is happening here, but I do know that this cult has a reach far longer than any of us know. I don't know what I would do if anything ever happened…"

He let the last few words go unspoken. Angelica only nodded in acknowledgement.

Ethan bent down, took the Khukuri blade, and put it into his belt. He did not want to be unarmed if there were more of the cultists out there.

They got themselves together and went back out of the tunnel and through the cabin. Walking past the table again, Ethan couldn't help but think that the bloodied leg of meat sitting there did *not* belong to a turkey. Angelica seemed to notice the same and voiced his unspoken thoughts.

"Those *aren't* turkey legs, are they?"

The fresh air was a welcome scent to them as they walked outside. They drove the horses at a furious gallop through the wind and rain until they got back to the ranch. Neither one of them spoke the entire ride back to the ranch.

Both hopped off their horses, took off the saddles, and put them back into the stables; making sure they had plenty of food and water. Angelica pulled over a small stool and motioned for Ethan to sit down.

"What for," questioned Ethan, "we don't have time to sit around!"

"Your arm; there's blood all over your shirt, let's at least get you bandaged up before an infection starts."

Ethan reluctantly sat down as Angelica went over to the small medicine cabinet hanging on the wall. She pulled out some cloth bandages, a bottle of alcohol, and a tube of anti-bacterial cream.

Walking back and kneeling down in front of Ethan, Angelica took his arm and carefully rolled up his sleeve to examine the wound. After a moment, she looked up at Ethan in utter shock. Her eyes like a frightened animal.

"Are you *sure* this is the arm that was cut," she asked, "There's barely a scratch here!"

"Of course; I think I'd know which arm was…" Ethan stopped suddenly as he looked at his arm.

She was right. There was a faint line where Red's knife had sliced him, but no visible wound or bleeding. His shirt was clearly bloodied, but maybe it had not even been *his* blood. Maybe it hadn't been as deep as he'd thought; but in the back of his mind, he knew that wasn't true. He rolled down his sleeve and stood up from the stool.

He had enough to worry about right now. Events had proceeded at such a climatic rate and he needed to keep up; there was no time for this.

Deep down, he knew something was wrong. Something was wrong with *him.*

"Ange...I need to get out of here..."

She looked at him in amazement.

"Ethan; what...does this mean?"

"I don't know."

He looked at himself in the mirror for a minute.

"Something happened to me in there, Ange. I couldn't *control* myself; I wanted to make them *pay* for what they did to that woman. This rage...it just overcame me and I knew exactly what I had to do. And now *this...*"

He looked down at his arm once more and ran both his hands through his face.

"I need to get to my condo, but first we need my laptop; it's back at your father's estate," said Ethan.

Angelica started to say something more about his arm, then thought better of it and let the subject drop. She was scared to death. Was it more of the Illuminati *or* the man that was next to her?

CHAPTER IV – REVELATIONS

They packed their things into the car and sped towards Christoph's mansion at over 90 miles per hour. Strange things were happening and they needed to get to the bottom of it fast. *Both of their lives* now depended on it.

Turning into the long driveway, Ethan pulled the car up to the front, jumped out and ran past the butler into the mansion. Angelica followed. The butler looked at them in anger and surprise.

"Sir, wait…"

"It's okay Henry," Angelica said to the butler, "I assume my father is not back yet?"

"No Ma'am, he will be tied up for one more day," stated the butler, "He has *requested* that both of you wait here until his return."

"*Fine* Henry," Angelica said hurriedly, "Please call him and tell him to get here as soon as he can! I *must* speak with him!"

"Ma'am, I…"

Angelica dismissed Henry with a wave of her hand and looked for Ethan. He must have already reached his room. She was right. He was packing up his things as she walked in. She closed the door behind her.

"Ethan," said Angelica, "I think you should show me the rest of that tape before we go any further. Whatever is happening here; somehow seems connected to Winehouse."

He looked at her in annoyance. They didn't have the time for this. At least not right now.

"Ange; we don't have…"

"Ethan; please…"

Ethan nodded back to her in agreement and motioned for her to sit down. He opened up his laptop and logged back in. He pushed play on the DVD to continue where he had left off.

Professor Winehouse's digitized features appearing on the screen was a welcome sight to Ethan. He missed his teacher terribly and was happy to see his face; even if he *were* only tiny bits of data.

"Most things do not happen out of coincidence, as most people assume; rather they are influenced for one reason or another. Look at our world today. We are manipulated by the media; a very *useful* tool of the Illuminati. The people are given only half of the story; the part they *want* you to hear. "

"Individualism is virtually non-existent; we are more like sheep, willingly lead to the slaughter. They have convinced us from *birth*, to focus on our faults and failures and how to become *more* than whom we are. What about our strengths and freedoms; what about accepting whom we *already* are; those traits are almost always overlooked. Wealth, power, materialistic things; those are what we need and crave to be fulfilled and in this, we have lost all hope and faith. In *this*, we have granted *them* control."

Winehouse paused to take a breath. He swept his white hair back from his eyes.

"All the wars; all the chaos; all the death – they have been manufactured by the Illuminati to take away our free will. Call it what you want: the Crusades; Fascism; Racism; Ignorance; whatever word may put it into perspective. It is all done to lead you astray; into the open and waiting arms of *evil*. They will accomplish this with false promises of peace, untold wealth, and unimaginable power. By accepting it, you *will forfeit* your very soul."

"Edward Burke said, 'The only thing necessary for evil to triumph is for good men to do nothing!'". He did not realize how true to life this was. "

The next part of the message took Ethan completely by surprise. It was directed at him. Onscreen, Professor Winehouse appeared to be staring right into his eyes. He moved closer to the camera.

"I leave this for you, Ethan Swan. *The answers lie within your self.* You do *not* have to follow the path they have laid before you. You can choose. Remember that. You *can choose.*"

With that, the screen went black.

Ethan backed up from the computer in disbelief. He hadn't expected the video message to be for *him*. Angelica was equally surprised.

"He...he said my name," Ethan exclaimed, "It was for *me*! What does he mean?!"

Ethan paced the room with his hands on his head. Winehouse must have known that something horrible may happen to him. Why had he not confided in anyone? Why did he simply leave this confusing legacy of a videotaped recording?

"I'm so sorry Ethan," soothed Angelica, "it seems like he may have been *expecting* this."

Anger welled up inside Ethan once more; he was visibly upset. He kicked the chair in frustration.

"Those bastards; he was *my friend*! I don't understand what he's trying to tell me."

"*The answers lie within your self,*" Angelica mused to herself, cryptically, "Why would he say something like that?"

Ethan ignored her comment, but appeared to have taken control of his emotions.

"We need to get to my condo; there's something *I need to see.*"

Angelica stayed silent; there was nothing more to say. Ethan packed up the laptop and his belongings, and then he and Angelica got back into the BMW and headed for the condo. It was two a.m. in the morning and the traffic was sparse. Neither one so much as glanced at the other, each drifting in separate thoughts of their own.

They were both exhausted as they pulled into the parking garage. Ethan led the way to his condo; Angelica close by his side. He put in his pass code and they stepped inside. He unhooked the knife from his belt and placed it on the table.

"We need some sleep," he urged, hoping she would follow his lead. Both of them headed straight for the bed and drifted off into a much needed slumber.

His dreams sped to him like the onset of a freight train. He was in front of a podium, surrounded by powerful diplomats and before a great audience of people. Other men were dressed in military attire; their medals glimmering off the sun off their well tailored uniforms.

Television News cameras were everywhere branding their symbols for the world to see. He recognized the logos from the US, but most of them were from other parts of the globe. Above them all waved an enormous flag signifying the 'new unity' of the civilized world.

A single golden eye streaming rays of light was stamped to the far left of the flag. Six stars symbolizing the leading few nations of the 195 independent countries of the planet Earth, stood out in a color of crimson red. To the right, there only remained an image of a black cross that seemed to be inverted just slightly enough to be noticed.

One of the gentlemen he was with, stepped forth to the microphone and waived his hand to silence the crowd. This man was notable for his deep scar running past his right cheek. He was also quite distinguished in his tailored suit and carried himself as being someone of importance.

"We are here today to usher forth a new era. The populace has made a *wise* choice in electing a leader as respected as Mr. Ethan Swan. This great man has brought us from the brink of chaos to the peaceful reign we have today. He has been an integral part of bringing us all together as a *world* society. Where we once had war; anger; murder; and distraught, we have now been united as one global community for the betterment of all humanity!"

The gathered crowd cheered as the cameras caught everything and broadcasted the conference across the continents.

"The Tri-mark Chip will be the very first multi-functional, digital data implant in the history of mankind! It will allow you to access all forms of financial, personal, and recorded information with the simple scan of your wrist. Security protocols are state of the art; completely firewalled, and only accessible through each individual's *unique genetic signature*. A painless inoculation, similar to a flu shot will be used to inject the chip into the bloodstream. We will begin the process world-wide, *immediately* after the conference!"

The crowd roared in response as the scene faded into another.

Black smoke spewed upwards from huge smokestacks, placed around large areas of barbed wire fencing. Fires burned from black pyres that were slowly corroding away. The statue of a large goat-like being, laid out in black steel stared out into the area. People; filthy and emaciated, were led like cattle towards a looming dark structure. Others were dragged, pushed, and beaten by what looked like soldiers or militia.

Guards with machine guns and ritual knives strapped to their waists were stationed on elevated platforms overlooking the grounds. Screams of agony and despair tore through the polluted air. An unknown voice came from an intercom in the distance, crackling as it spoke.

"Those that are unbelievers of the dark god and deny his gifts will be terminated upon discovery. As always, you will be given a choice to *convert* before reaching the Chamber. Think of your loved ones; think of the riches; think of the power; they can *all* be yours if you have *faith*!"

The view of the horrors faded into black. He thought he heard himself scream somewhere in the black nothingness. He slept.

Ethan woke up to the smell of bacon, eggs, and homemade blueberry pancakes. Angelica was standing above him with a ready-made breakfast plate. She looked even cuter with her tousled hair and wearing nothing else but one of his tailored shirts.

"Good Morning handsome," she said with a smile, "or should I say afternoon."

Ethan turned his head to look over at the clock; it was indeed close to 1:30 in the afternoon. He reached for the plate and hungrily inhaled the food.

"Thanks Ange, I'm starving," he managed to mumble between the mouthfuls.

She sat down next to him and waited patiently until he was done. She reached over and dabbed his mouth with a napkin.

"Maybe we should get in a shower to wake you up," she said playfully, "come on."

She dragged him into the bathroom and turned on the water in the decorative shower. The spray of water reminded him of their recent encounter by the waterfall. He soon realized that she must have remembered the same. She pushed him into the stall and forced his hand to her breasts.

"Ange; wait…I don't…"

"Not this time, okay…I want to."

Ethan gently pushed her in and kissed her deeply. She returned his passion by roughly pushing him against the tile and raking her nails down his back. Lust took over as they made frantic love in the wet confines of the stall; the spray coming down on their bodies like rain.

They stepped out of the shower stall and back in the bedroom, they did it once more. Finally exhausted from their wild throes of passion, they held each other close for a few moments.

Ethan looked down upon Angelica's naked body and saw that sleep had claimed her into its own soft embrace. He felt…relieved. He had always wondered what would happen if it had ever gotten this far. Would he feel different towards her, somehow ashamed to break a friendship, angry at allowing himself to get personal?

Peering down into her beautiful face, these thoughts did not matter anymore. He felt as if they had always been together; they *belonged* together. He would not see her harmed in any way! Gently placing her head onto the pillow, he got out of bed and pulled on his pants and shirt. He *would* find a way to save them; regardless of the cost.

Ethan walked out into the living room and took a seat on the expensive leather couch. While waiting for Angelica to wake, he thought over the increasingly strange events that had taken place in his life. All these things were somehow connected.

He went to his office desk and pulled out the flash device and the small notebook from the hidden compartment underneath. There *has* to be something here, he thought to himself.

He rifled through the pages slowly in the dead detective's notebook. Some of the pages had familiar markings on them:

: The Swastika- most people did not know that it was an ancient occult symbol of the sun. The Nazis had taken it and twisted it into a symbol that was feared throughout the world.

: Nero's Cross- commonly known as the piece symbol, but in reality, a broken, upside-down cross deeply rooted to signify the destruction of Christianity.

 : The Pentagram- used in occult rituals to direct forces or energies often represents Satanism or evil.

Other pages in the notebook were blank. One page in particular had a name and date: Ulric Fe – June 6th, 2006. Ethan understood immediately. It was an anagram. He had been taught the hidden meanings of signs and symbols from his father, Earl Swan. *It was an anagram for Lucifer, 666.* But, what did it mean?

"What did you find?"

Ethan jumped; startled and looked up to see that Angelica had woken up and come back into the room.

"Damn; don't do that Ange, you scared the *shit* out of me!"

"Did you find something," she pressed.

"I don't know. Maybe, this whole thing…is really driving me *crazy*," he replied, wavering.

"I know. You didn't sleep very well last night; you were having nightmares."

"I had a very bizarre dream last night; I feel like I may be a part of something I obviously don't understand! It almost seemed like I was looking at a future version of myself and I was involved in something *terrible*."

"Ethan..."

"Just listen Ange, let me explain," he said, stopping her abruptly.

Ethan pulled Angelica down, to sit beside him and began to describe the details of his dream to her. He told her everything he could remember. As he finished, Angelica seemed unsettled. He didn't blame her.

"*Why* would you be a part of *them?* They were *using* you Ethan; *controlling* you somehow! It wasn't you; don't you see?"

"Ange, it seemed as if most of the world was *willing* participants in all of this. Why would anyone give in to *their* sick views," he asked, almost speaking to himself. In his heart, he knew. Money; glory; power: people wanted these things; even he and Angelica weren't much different. Who didn't want to be rich and powerful? The choice, however, would come down to how far someone was willing to go to obtain those things. Would someone give up their very soul for a few years of happiness? Not him and certainly not Angelica!

He remembered the concentration camps. There were more people than just him that would not give up hope. Regardless of threats or even death, there were those that truly believed in God and would fight the Illuminati; down to their last breaths.

"Ethan; hey, are you okay," asked Angelica, bringing him from his thoughts.

"Sorry, I was just thinking."

"Listen, this…Tri-mark Chip; you mentioned that Winehouse had talked about some kind of smart card. Could it be real?"

Ethan thought about it for a minute. Yes, it could very well be true. What better way for the cult to exert control over people than keeping a leash on their very livelihoods. The chip would have direct control over buying, selling, trading, GPS, even personal or business information. The people of the world had taken so much for granted for so long and now their total dominance would come in the form of a highly advanced microchip.

"I don't know if that is what it will be called, but I do know that even now, some major credit card companies are developing these so-called bio-chips. The information is very scarce, but it's there if you know where to look. The more technology improves, the less we have control of it."

Angelica's face was a canvas of deep thought. She was putting all of her effort into finding some kind of answer as to why these people were doing this. In his heart, Ethan knew there would never be a rational explanation for the cult's desire for Armageddon.

"Okay, just stay with me for a minute," she said finally, "you were saying that most people had sided with the Illuminati; do you really think they would do that, even knowing that satan would control their lives?"

Ethan looked at her with sadness. Sometimes, she was so naïve. Her extravagant lifestyle had eluded her to most people's wants and needs.

"Ange, I saw this movie once, about the end of the world. Men, women, children; even families were infiltrated, fattened up on lies, and granted some sort of psychic-type power. These people embraced it; as if it was a gift on Christmas Day!"

Ethan paused to make sure she was attentive.

"In one scene, this young man comes back to his family's home and his father is waiting for him with a smile on his face. The family had already succumbed to the Mark of the Beast and the father was tasked with either converting his son or eliminating him. His father had a gun under a blanket by his chair; fully cocked and loaded. He welcomed his son with open arms and sat him down to explain his reasons for converting."

Ethan's eyes filled with despair as he took a deep breath. Angelica was listening intently.

"When his son refused to hear his lies, the father told him to wait and watch the television screen. After about five minutes of intense concentration, the television turned on by itself and flipped through the channels of its own accord. The son, of course was shocked. His

118 | P a g e

father continued to enlighten him on the *power* he was given by the devil for his allegiance."

"Not to interrupt; and I am merely being the 'devil's advocate', so to speak," stated Angelica, "but power like that would really give people a *reason* to convert to their ideals, don't you think?"

"Maybe so, but I'm not finished. After witnessing this, the son turned off the television and asked his father to do it again. The father complied and began to concentrate. Meanwhile, his son stood up, reached for the remote control and turned the TV & flipped through the channels in a matter of seconds. He looked at his father and said, 'If you would sell your soul for a matter of convenience, then you are better off dead!' and with that he backed out of the door keeping the gun he had taken, pointed at his father. That young man went on to start a revolution against the antichrist and his followers. He had *faith*."

Angelica looked as if she was distraught.

"My God, Ethan, is that what Winehouse meant; about having a choice; about *you*?"

"Maybe; maybe he wanted to let me know that I can *do something* to change all of this. Everyone has a choice, Ange; between good and evil, right and wrong, whatever you want to call it. But, why me; I'm no one special…"

"Ethan, after all we've seen today, I've seen how *special* you are. It's the *rest* of the world I'm concerned about."

He stared at her for a minute, contemplating in silent thought.

"We are sheep Ange," he said solemnly, "most times, we *follow* the many; not *lead* the few."

"Every so often, you really impress me," she replied with a smile.

Ethan silently got up and grasped his coat. He reached into the pocket and pulled out a small plastic bag, containing the metal shard he had found on the woman cultist. He placed it on the table, in front of Angelica.

"I took this from the woman who killed the Professor. I think I know what it is."

"It looks familiar for some reason," Angelica replied.

"It should," stated Ethan, "It fits into this"

Ethan took the metal shard out of the bag and attached it to the strange flash drive. It was a perfect fit. Exactly like the one he found on Red, he thought to himself.

Angelica got up, retrieved the laptop from the bedroom and sat back down next to Ethan.

"Here," she said, "let's see what's on this thing!"

Ethan logged in and inserted the flash drive. The computer went blank, and then reappeared again with the word 'CLASSIFIED' in large red letters. Below that, it said 'Authorized User Access Only' with a space on the right for what was obviously for a password of some sort.

"Now what," Angelica inquired.

"Give me a minute," replied Ethan, as he closed his eyes and looked up to the ceiling in deep thought.

There were seven blank spaces for a password. He had taken the flash drive off the detective. S-A-M-A-E-L – that was only six. He perused that for a minute and reached for Samael's notebook. He scanned through the pages again; Ulric Fe:

Lucifer! He typed in the word: L-U-C-I-F-E-R and hit 'ENTER'. The flash drive whirred to life and words instantly appeared on the screen: 'ACCESS GRANTED'.

It opened up, listing four separate files on the computer. Ethan and Angelica simultaneously took a breath, preparing themselves for the unknown.

The first file had a name on it: Project Morning Son; S-O-N, not S-U-N. Ethan opened the file. It appeared on the screen amidst a backdrop of an inverted Pentacle:

The Pentacle was similar to a Pentagram; however, it was enclosed by a circle, symbolizing eternity, totality, and unity. It is said that the inversion represented the drawing of the energy of the spirit into the physical body.

A page of statistical-like information spewed forth. It appeared in the style of some type of medical chart.

PROJECT MORNING SON: [CLASSIFIED]

SUBJECT D114:   Ethan Damian Swan

CURRENT PHYSICAL DESCRIPTION:

Hair: Brown; Eyes: Black; Height-Six Feet, 0 inches; Weight-180 lbs

Peak physical condition; enhanced intelligence; mentally stable

GENETIC ENHANCEMENTS:

➢ Genius Intellect

➢ Heightened Awareness

➢ Photographic Retention

➢ Accelerated Healing

➢ Enhanced Strength

POJECT AWAKEN DATE: December 21st, 2012

STATUS: Memory Blocks: Shattered upon Surrogate Caretaker's Death

ADVISED [issued 1/6/2011]: Subject **Not Ready** for Complete Awakening:

Programming Incomplete

Consider Extremely Dangerous

-FIND AND TERMINATE WITH EXTREME PREJUDICE...

AUTHENTICATION: PRIME ALPHA –TFCN

END.

"Oh my God," Angelica exclaimed, "Ethan..."

Ethan reeled back from the laptop in utter shock. He jumped up in fear and self-loathing, picking up a small end table and throwing it across the room.

It collided against the far wall of the living room; tearing a hole, exposing cable wire that spidered upwards into the drywall. He placed a well-rounded kick to the Beansac, puncturing the side; small micro-beads spilling out.

"Ethan," Angelica started to say, terrified at his sudden outburst.

His face was flushed; nostrils flaring. She had never seen him like this.

"What the FUCK AM I," Ethan screamed, "WHAT did they do to me?!"

"Ethan, please," Angelica said as she came to his side, palms outstretched; signaling for him to calm down," this isn't helping!"

Ethan looked at her; hands by his mouth, and forced himself to relax. He took a few deep breaths; hands on his head and walked into her open arms. Sobbing quietly, he managed to hold her while he composed himself. Silently, Angelica held him. A few minutes later, Ethan collected himself and let his arms slip away.

"Ange…I…I'm not that thing. I..I'm still ME!"

"I don't care what you are," Angelica replied soothingly, "They don't *control* you and that's what they are afraid of."

Ethan had finally calmed himself down. He appeared composed, yet Angelica could see that an anger burned in him, deep inside. It wanted *out.*

"They've done something to me! If it's the killer they want; it's a *killer* I'll give them!"

"We need to see the rest of it," she prompted, sitting back down in front of the laptop.

Ethan relaxed himself, took a few deep breaths, and sat down beside her. He surveyed the screen. There were three other files remaining: 'E-Swan', 'D114', and 'Vid1'. He opened up the first one: 'E-Swan'.

An image of his father, Earl Swan, came up on the screen. He hadn't seen a picture of his father since the accident. He had preferred to remember him in his memories, rather than be reminded of his untimely death, so he had put his photos into boxes and stored them in his attic.

Underneath the photograph, there were intimate details about his father: his physical statistics, his numerous degrees and doctorates, family history, and so on. What caught his eye was a small text box off to the lower right hand corner of the screen. In bold, red text, it said

'DESIGNATE: Surrogate Caretaker/Handler – SCHEDULED FOR TERMINATION: **AUTHENTICATION: PRIME ALPHA –TFCN'**

Ethan choked on his breath. What the hell did that mean? Was it implying that Earl Swan wasn't his real father? Did the hierarchy of the Illuminati want his father killed for some reason?

"WHY would your *father* be in here," questioned Angelica.

"It designates him as a 'Surrogate Caretaker'; I don't even know if he *is* my father anymore! From everything we've seen so far, it seems like my entire life has been a lie from the beginning!"

"Ethan, even *if* Earl Swan was *not* your biological father; which remains to be seen, the man raised you from birth as his own son; to me, he more than qualifies as *your* father!"

Ethan wavered in anger before he answered.

"You're right Ange; he was always there for me, in his own way. He was a great man," Ethan paused, letting it all sink in, "but just *how* is he involved in all of this?"

"I wish I had an answer for you," she replied, "this...*conspiracy* only worsens as we go on!"

"*That* is an understatement; what do we do now?"

"We keep going," she stated, abruptly.

Angelica put her finger on the mouse pad and clicked on the next file: 'D114'.

Ethan retained that this was his 'subject number' from Project Morning Son. As he expected, it was an informational document like his father's. It again, implied that Ethan Swan was not entirely human; more like an experiment gone wrong.

Appearing at the bottom was the same marking:

'SCHEDULED FOR TERMINATION: **AUTHENTICATION: PRIME ALPHA –TFCN'**

However, in place of the description on his father's notary, it said,

'DESIGNATE: D114 – ENHANCED HUMAN RESEARCH'.

He looked at Angelica as she stared back, knowingly. Neither one said a word.

The last file: 'Vid1' opened up to a video recording of an unknown man. He looked and was dressed like a scientist, except for the obvious '6-66' emblem on his lab coat. He was a small, frail gentleman, but his eyes were blank; no emotion came forth from them. Behind him was some sort of computerized cocoon; a chamber big enough for a human being. His voice, as he spoke, was monotone as if he was an inert encyclopedia stating facts.

"From birth, onwards to the age of six years, we have found that the human mind is an open book. The subconscious can be easily manipulated to accept electronic data input. However, the subject must be *programmed* in an isolated environment to fully utilize the results of the procedure. To this effect, we have developed an artificial womb in the form of a highly advanced sensory deprivation chamber, code-named 'Deep Sleep One'."

"The absence of outside stimuli allows us to effectively program the brain, much akin to downloading information onto a computer. The compound, **Genome6-66** is introduced to the subject intravenously. We have found that; over repetitive treatments, it has the ability to greatly enhance both physical and mental attributes, at an accelerated rate."

The scientist was interrupted by another man for a moment. It looked as if he was signing something, and then he continued.

"The absence of light, sound, and interaction awakens the **Pineal Gland**. *This*, coupled with extended periods in the isolation chamber accomplishes two things: the Pineal Gland produces very high levels of melatonin, causing the subject to enter an absolute hibernation; and in the process, opens a doorway into what is known as the '**Soul**'. "

Ethan and Angelica watched and listened, as their skin prickled in fear and dread.

"Three subjects were chosen, based on specific physical criteria and historic bloodlines, leading back to 100 B.C. Out of three, two experienced extreme mental exertion and were reduced to vegetative states. Termination of these subjects was authorized by the Company. The remaining subject: **D114**, a.k.a. Ethan Swan, exhibited superior physical and mental abilities. Subject D114 is the end result of **Project Morning Son**."

With that last statement, the video ended abruptly.

Ethan blinked in disbelief and awe. Flashes came to him in the facts of realization. The dreams he'd had, since he was young, of 'being in a coffin' were immediately explained. His high intelligence; his uncanny awareness; the reason he was so quick to learn and pick things up; the fact that he was hardly ever sick; it all made sense instantly.

Angelica looked pale; mouth wide open and still as a statue.

"Ange, are...are you okay," asked Ethan, snapping out of his reverie.

She slowly turned to look at him; fear outlining her face. Her face was as white as a ghost.

"Yeah...yeah, I'm fine."

She took his hands in hers and she turned to face him. A single tear slipped down her delicate features.

"I'm with you always, you know; no matter *whom* you are."

"If you need some space, I understand," Ethan replied, "I..would feel the same if..."

"Are you really that dense," she interrupted, "I've loved you since we were kids!"

Ethan felt a great relief in his heart. He pulled her towards him and held her tightly. He was certain that she would have felt frightened by him; he knew he was.

"Thank you Ange…I know this is not how you expected it to be."

Ethan kept her close to him as his mind wandered. Who did this to him? Why did they do it? Why did they kill his father? What was he capable of? The last of these questions seemed to immediately bother him. He remembered the way he had lost control of himself and the burning rage he had felt in the cave. Would he be a danger to Angelica? Could he be capable of hurting her?

He stared at the hole in the wall and the damage he had done. The leg of the end table had gone right through the drywall and the wires were nakedly exposed. How was he going to cover up those wires? Wires; what were wires doing in the wall?

Ethan gently pushed Angelica over to the side and stood up. He walked towards the exposed cables. They ran upwards about two feet, towards one of the heat vents. He took a closer look at them for a minute or so, and then walked over to the mini-bar.

"What are you *doing*," asked Angelica, straightening herself on the couch.

Ethan didn't reply. He pulled open a draw, took out a large metal screwdriver, and then moved a bar stool over to the wall.

"Ethan!"

"Give me a minute, Ange."

He got up on the stool and pushed the screwdriver into one of the holes in the grate. He pushed it upwards to force open the cover. The grate came crashing to the ground, with a loud clang. He took out his tiny penlight attached to his key chain and shined it into the hole.

About 6 inches into the darkness, he saw a tiny metallic device; a transmitter of some sort, attached to the wires running down his wall. When he was younger, he had used a similar device to listen in on his father's business talks; just for fun. This time, it looked as if the tables had been turned.

He got down from the stool and saw Angelica fidgeting in her seat; she was looking at him curiously. He reached out and grabbed her hand, pulling her towards him.

"We need to get out of here – NOW!"

"What are you…"

Ethan cut her off with a finger to her lips and bent down to whisper in her ear. He pointed to the wires showing through the wall as he spoke.

"Whatever those wires are, they sure don't belong to any *speaker system*; someone's been listening to us. Get your things."

Ethan quickly reached for his laptop and brought the screen down in place. He unplugged the flash drive, grabbed the notebook off the table and placed them into his pack. He went back into the bedroom, wiped the Khukuri blade clean, and placed it back into his belt. He had a feeling he may need some kind of protection. Angelica gathered her things just as fast. Five minutes later, they were both out the door.

Taking the elevator down to the parking garage, Ethan was feeling uneasy. His mind whirled with questions. How long had that device been there? Have they been listening to everything that was said? Who was on the other end?

The elevator came to an abrupt and screeching stop. The doors opened and he and Angelica walked out into the garage. The lights were dimmer than usual. He looked about warily and noticed that a light was out above his parking stall. He turned his head, viewing the expanse of the garage and saw nothing, but the parked cars.

It seemed safe. He took a hold of Angelica's hand and slowly led her towards his car. As they walked, he clicked the unlock button on his keys. In the distance, the lights on the BMW blinked on and off.

Ethan turned his head sharply toward the sudden noise of footsteps. It approached from the way they had just come from. He started to remove the knife as the person or something walked into the light. He promptly slid the knife back into his belt.

"Hey there sexy," came the voice of Cassie Parker, his beautiful neighbor across the hall.

She was dressed in a low-cut black dress; showing off her creamy thighs; her red flat shoes looked out of place. Her long hair was pulled up in a bun and her hips swayed sinfully as she walked slowly towards him, looking as gorgeous as ever. An expensive looking coat adorned her upper body and came down halfway past her hips.

"Cassie," Ethan exclaimed, "What the hell are you doing here?!"

"I *live* here asshole, or don't you remember," she smirked, looking in the direction of Angelica.

Ethan stepped forward and between them, feeling a bit sheepish. Please don't let her say anything to Ange about me, he thought to himself. All he needed was an all-out cat fight to break out between the two lovely ladies.

"What do we *have* here," Cassie said rhetorically.

Ethan cleared his throat. Just then, he would have rather been back in the cave.

"Ange, this is Cassie Turner; she's my neighbor from across the hall."

"I'm Angelica," she stated, introducing herself with an outstretched hand.

Cassie ignored Angelica's gesture of introduction, with a wave of her hand. She turned and looked at Ethan annoyingly.

"Bitch," Angelica muttered under her breath.

"Where have you been," Cassie accused Ethan, "I stopped over at your place the other day and you weren't home *again*."

"Anywhere but here; I've tried to stay away from this place," Ethan replied, "Haven't you heard what happened?"

"Yes, I have. I do read the paper, you know? I've been a little scared myself with all these cult freaks around. Why don't we go up to my place and you can fill me in on exactly what has been happening with you lately."

"Cassie, I…"

Ethan broke off in mid-sentence, and then looked at Cassie. How did she know?

"What did you say," he started again.

"I said, leave the skank here and come upstairs with me!"

Ethan reached for the blade in his belt and brandished the knife before him. Angelica watched in silence as she stepped back.

Cassie Turner stared back at the weapon and smiled; a wicked grin altering her delicate features. She reached behind her coat and pulled out an exact replica of the Khukuri Knife Ethan was holding. She licked her lips slowly.

"If you want to get *kinky*; then so can I," she purred as she held the blade at length.

Ethan wasn't surprised. He watched her closely for any sign of movement as he twirled the blade in his hand. They stared at each other for a moment; each one watching to see who would strike first. Cassie laughed tauntingly.

"I don't suppose you would want to put these down and go upstairs with me, would you? It could be like old times!"

She laughed again. She knew how to get under his skin.

"Sure," Ethan said calmly, "You first."

Ethan looked over at Angelica. She was staring at him with angry eyes. Cassie noticed.

"Don't worry about the little whore," Cassie screamed, "She means *nothing*!"

"Ethan," Angelica shouted to him.

Cassie leapt for him with a swipe of her knife. He turned his stomach inward, narrowly missing the edge of the sharp blade.

She backed up a bit and started circling him.

"Fool; you could have had it *all* and you blew it," Cassie said, eyes bulging, "and for *what*? That little *bitch*? Your *senile* professor; or maybe it was your *traitor* father!?"

Ethan didn't reply. His mind was going through multiple scenarios to find the best tactic to win.

Cassie darted back in for another swing, as Ethan turned his body at the same time. Dodging to the right, he brought his knife arm, blade down, and slashed downwards. He made contact with the side of her chest. It was a superficial cut at best, but the blood forming under her clothing clearly showed that he had hit his mark.

She didn't even wince as she stabbed towards his neck. He tilted his head and upper body back as he saw the sharp instrument reaching just inches from his neck. Ethan turned slightly, bringing his left hand to slam against her armed hand. It caused her to move to the side. He pivoted his footing and brought around a swift kick from a powerful leg.

His kick caught her in the square of her spine as this time, she grunted in pain.

Amazingly, Cassie went back with the force of the kick, rolled forward and jumped back up in a fighting stance. She got up about eight feet in front of him.

She was a professional assassin, he surmised. She seemed to be used to pain and her reflexes were unbelievable. The strange look on her face was surprisingly of sorrow.

Cassie took him by surprise with her next move. She ran straight for him and with a quick swipe, managed to slice him above his left collarbone. Ethan grimaced in pain and jumped back.

Angelica cried out. Damn her concern! She still hadn't backed up.

The wetness of the seeping blood focused his attention back to the fight.

"Oooh, baby," she said with a smile, "did I *cut* you?"

The mad woman brought the bloodied knife to her mouth and with a long, sexy swipe of her tongue, licked it clean.

"It's okay," Ethan taunted back, "It *seems* I heal fast."

Angelica started to sob quietly in the background. She was unsure of what to do amidst all the chaos.

Cassie smiled wickedly at him.

"I've just about had *enough* of your whining bitch!"

Cassie started moving towards Angelica; all the while keeping a sharp eye on Ethan.

Ethan could feel the rage boiling up in him as he ran for Cassie. He was cold and calculating, as he brought down his knife across her side. Cassie attempted to move out of harm's way, but was too slow. Wincing in pain, she kneed Ethan in the kidneys. He recovered quickly and came at her again.

The metal of the two knifes clashed to the sound of a deadly symphony as the two battled. Small sparks flew in the darkness of the parking structure. They each dodged; countered; and moved to the beat of a dance of death.

Ethan grabbed Cassie by the arm and deflected a blow. He then brought his blade down quickly into the small of her back. Blood burst forth in a red, sticky stream. Cassie's hand let go of her knife and she fell to the ground in a heap. She was coughing up a small amount of blood, but her lips were snarled in a sick, twisted smile. Ethan bent down and grabbed her by the hair.

"*Who* wants me dead," he began, "Who the hell are you people? What do you know of my *father*?!"

Angelica started moving towards them.

"Ange," Ethan yelled, "stay back!"

He looked down at Cassie. She was trying to talk. Red spittle framed the corners of her mouth.

"For...old time's sake," she sputtered, "...Doctor Armin...Zolof."

"Thank you Cassie," he said, gently placing her head down.

He turned to get up as Cassie grabbed him by the arm.

"Ethan…they…know…*everything*," she said as her eyes rolled up and died.

She was right, he pondered. He suddenly realized what that meant. It was her. The wires in his house; the transmitter; she had been placed there to gather information. If he was correct, the rest of the sick bastards knew everything he and Angelica had discussed at the condo. In fact, who knew how long they'd been listening. He glanced over to Angelica.

Watching this all take place, Angelica was a nervous wreck. She reached for her cell phone and dialed a number.

"What are you doing," Ethan asked.

"We…we need to call…the police," she stammered back.

"No," he stated.

Not this time. Ethan knew that with the multiple instances he had been at the 'murder scenes', the cops would have no choice but to put him in jail on a temporary basis; at least until the truth was uncovered. He did not have the time for that right now; not when he was *so close* to the truth.

He stood up and pulled Angelica into his arms. He looked her in the eyes and tried to explain the reasons for not calling the cops. Understanding slowly crept over her face.

"We need to go," he stated.

Angelica let go of his shoulders and nodded. Ethan picked up both blades and walked to the BMW. He opened the trunk and tossed them in. He took a moment to gather himself.

Once he got into the car, he began to look over everything, searching for anything that seemed out of place. If they had wired his condo, they must have done the same to his car. He ripped out anything electronic that was not held down and threw it out of the car.

"Ethan," Angelica broke the silence, "How did you know about her?"

He looked directly in front, avoiding her gaze.

"The papers said nothing about them being *cultists*."

CHAPTER V – TRUTH

He put the car in reverse and they pulled out into the awaiting street. It had started to rain.

It had gotten considerably darker outside, Ethan noticed as he pulled the sports car onto the freeway. They needed a place to think things through. They obviously couldn't go back to the condo and it would be a bad idea to head to Angelica's. Besides, he didn't want to get Christoph involved in all of this crazy shit.

That left a motel. Ethan exited the off ramp and turned down Roden Street. It was an isolated area and he knew of a few places to stay for the night.

He noticed that Angelica had stayed silent the entire drive. He held his concern for her and contemplated their next move.

Ethan found a place called the 'Starlight Motel' on the west side of Roden Street. It looked old and dingy, but it was perfect. It wasn't a national chain or well known, where someone would have a hard time tracking them down.

He turned the car into the open expanse of the parking lot and managed to squeeze the BMW in between a camper and a large truck. They were concealed well, but could be noticed if someone were to walk through the lot. He didn't see that happening; after all, they had not spoken about where they were going back at the condo.

Ethan put the car into park and gazed at Angelica. Even as scared as she was, she still looked beautiful. He hoped she wasn't in shock.

"Angelica," he started, "Are you going to be okay?"

She turned from watching the rain beat against the window, towards Ethan.

"You *never* call me Angelica."

"I'm sorry Ange," he said soothingly, "This is not what I had in mind for us."

"I *know* Ethan," she replied, "It's just that when she started coming for me, I got a good look at her eyes. She wasn't crazy; she was fanatical! She truly believed in what she was about to do; she reveled in it; she wanted it."

She paused to look at him.

"What I'm trying to say is that, whoever these people are; *this* Illuminati, they won't *stop* until we're both dead, or they are!"

Ethan took her hand and pulled her in close.

"I promise you," he swore, "I won't let anything happen to you. I have a feeling we're *very close* to figuring this all out."

He let her go and opened the door.

"Wait here."

Ethan reached under the seat and opened a compartment hidden below. He pulled out a wad of cash, wrapped in a rubber band, and then headed for the motel. He put on his coat, hoping to hide the still wet blood congealing by his shoulder.

Soaking with rain, he opened the door and walked in. The man at the front desk was an ugly oaf. Ethan could smell the sweat of unwashed clothes as he walked towards him. He grabbed a few fifty dollar bills out of the wad and tossed it to him.

"I need a room."

The man reached under the desk and brought up a hotel register. He took the money and gave Ethan a pen.

"Sign your name here. You have Room 28D."

Ethan picked up the pen and wrote down a random name: William Right

"*Nobody* knows I'm here," stated Ethan as he threw down another fifty dollars.

"You got it."

Ethan opened the door and went back to the car to get Angelica. She had already retrieved his backpack and laptop and was heading his way. He motioned for her to follow him and they walked past the office and around the corner to Room 28D. Ethan opened the door and they walked in. Both of them were soaked & cold from the rain.

The room was a standard motel room. The old, faded walls looked like they hadn't been washed in ages. The bed was a queen and a small television and phone were placed invitingly on the dresser. The worn carpeting had an odor coming from it, emanating into the rest of the room. A small bathroom was off to the left, which happened to be the only place that actually looked clean.

Ethan headed to the bathroom and came back with some towels. He handed one to Angelica and sat on the bed to dry off. He peeled back his shirt to take a look at his wound. As he had thought, there was now only an open, bloodied scratch where once a deep gash had been. He was finally beginning to understand that this may be a gift; not a curse.

"What now," she asked.

"*Now*, we find out what we can on this Doctor Zoloff," he replied and plugged in his laptop and turned it on. He logged in and opened up the network access screen. Angelica threw her towel on the floor and joined him on the bed.

His wireless card picked up an unsecured network close by, allowing him close to three bars of bandwidth. Ethan brought up his internet search browser and typed in: Doctor Armen Zoloff, Boston MA. It brought up a query asking him if he had meant: Doctor Armin Zolof, Boston Massachusetts, so he clicked on the correct spelling.

A number of search results came up, going back to the late-sixties. The most recent of them was an article that said, 'Metacorp Laboratories Recruits World Renowned Geneticist'. Ethan clicked on it and skimmed through the article.

'BOSTON MA--Metacorp laboratories proudly welcomes Doctor Armin Zolof, a top-level Geneticist. Some may remember Dr. Zolof from the controversial court trial during the early-eighties, where he was accused of tampering with the genetic structure of human genes. Time seems to have made amends for Zolof who was recruited by Metacorp last month...'

Ethan stopped reading and went further back and found the article that was mentioned previously. This one read, 'Geneticist Faces Prosecution for Human Experimentation'. He opened it and read through carefully.

'Houston TX—A brilliant Geneticist may face federal prosecution today for human gene altering and the deaths of two people. Dr. Armin Zolof claims that he has found the fountain of youth. He calls the compound Genome6-66. The two human test subjects, he says volunteered of their own free will and knew the risks involved. The Doctor says he can produce the signed waivers if need be.

According to Zolof, Genome6-66 was an experimental serum that could actually change the genetic make-up of a normal human gene. With the right stimuli, the physical and mental enhancements of the drug could produce a PERFECT human being.

Genome6-66 has the potential to make a person stronger, faster, and smarter in a matter of years says Zolof. His trial is set to begin next week.'

Ethan did a search on the doctor's name using an image selection. The image popped up immediately. Ethan was not surprised; the picture was identical to the scientist in the video he and Angelica had watched on the flash drive. This picture showed a younger Doctor Zolof; his cold, dead eyes still remained the same, even after all these years.

As he was examining the picture, he heard a musical ringing. It was coming from Angelica. She reached into her pocket and flipped open the cell phone.

"Hello?'

"Who is it," Ethan demanded.

"It's okay, it's my father."

"Put him on speaker."

"Okay," she answered, "Dad, just a minute."

Angelica pushed the speaker button on her phone and placed it on the small desk.

"Dad, are you still there; can you hear me?"

"Yes Honey; Will Hicks called me. He said you and Ethan had come down to the ranch to take the horses out, and then just *disappeared* before morning!"

"Ummm…Dad," started Angelica without finishing.

"Uncle Christoph, it's me Ethan. We've got you on speaker phone. We had to leave unexpectedly; something came up."

"Ethan, are you two okay? Is everything alright?"

Ethan touched Angelica and put a finger to his lips.

"We're fine. We're just spending some time together at my place; you know, catching up on old times. We'll be back to see you tomorrow night," he lied.

"Okay, okay. Listen; I spoke with Chief Stroh," replied Christoph, "He assures me that you have nothing to worry about. He said he can assign two officers for around the clock protection. They will be by your side, wherever you go."

"That's great news; I'll speak to him when I get back."

"Thank you so much Dad," Angelica broke in.

"Anytime, sweetheart," Christoph answered, "I'm so sorry for the sudden rush; you know how business calls. Look, I'll see you both when you get here, okay? I love you guys; be good!"

As the line on the other end hung up, Angelica looked inquisitively at Ethan.

"Why didn't you tell him the truth?"

"Ange, I'm sorry; It's better that he doesn't know. The less involved he is with all of this, the safer he'll be. The last thing I need is for your father to get hurt because of *me*!"

"You're right," she said, as she moved in and hugged him. He reciprocated the hug and held her close for a few minutes. She obviously needed it. He was amazed at this woman who had stuck by his side, even after all the hell they'd just experienced.

"Maybe this Doctor can help us find out what happened to you," she spoke softly.

Ethan let her go and took another look at Doctor Armin Zolof's image on the computer. The previous article had said he now worked for Metacorp Laboratories. Metacorp was located about forty minutes in the industrial quarters of Boston.

"We can't go there like this," he said, looking at himself in the large mirror atop the dresser.

He put on his coat, grabbed the car keys and headed for the door. He turned back to Angelica.

"What size are you," he asked Angelica.

"Size one," she replied.

"I'll be right back," he said, stepping out the door, "Don't answer the door to *anyone*, unless you're *sure* it's me."

Ethan walked back to the car and started the engine. If they were going to somehow approach this Doctor, they certainly couldn't go dressed like this.

He pulled out into Roden Street, and then drove a few miles to Main. He turned the car and came into the downtown district. He chose a privately-held place of business rather than a large department store, hoping to avoid any security cameras or someone recognizing him.

Twenty minutes later, he came out of the store with a black suit, tie, and matching shoes in one hand. In the other, he carried a grey and tan women's business suit, complete with a purse and high heels; size one.

Ethan got back into the car and drove up another block. He pulled into the drive-thru of a fast food restaurant and ordered himself and Angelica some much needed food. After that, he put the car in drive and sped away, back to the hotel.

Knocking at the faded wooden entrance of Room 28D, he was relieved to hear Angelica ask who was at the door. He had assumed that she would open the door right away; obviously, she was right on top of things, smart girl.

"It's me," he replied.

"I don't know who 'me' is," came the reply.

"I have *food*."

The door opened immediately and Ethan laughed. She had definitely returned to normal; the earlier fear and doubt had vanished from her face. Her look of confidence overcame his doubts.

"About damn time you do something useful," she smirked, "Is that for me?"

Ethan passed the outfit over to her. He could see, by the look on her face that she approved. She sat the clothes down on the bed and rushed to the bags of food.

They were both famished. Angelica had inhaled two burgers, before Ethan had a chance to finish even his first. She tore through the brown paper bags, taking handfuls of French Fries and shoving them into her mouth. He followed her lead and filled himself with enough of the fatty, greasy food, that weariness soon overcame him.

They slept well. No nightmares came to Ethan that night. He slept in peace, regardless of the fear of what the next day may bring.

Waking up later that morning, Ethan felt rather invigorated. Angelica was next to him; mouth open and snoring loudly. Ethan laughed to himself and nudged her awake. He looked over to the dresser and noticed that he had left his laptop on through the night.

He got out of bed and went to the bathroom. After taking a shower, he came back to the room to find Angelica was awake and busy removing her new outfit from the plastic bag. She noticed him behind her and turned to face him.

"I assume this is to go to Metacorp," she asked rhetorically, pointing to the attire.

"We need to look professional," Ethan replied, "Why don't you get in the shower?"

"You don't need to tell me twice," she said, getting up and pecking him on the lips. She took her clothes with her.

Ethan toweled dry and put on his suit. He admired his new, professional look in the mirror. He was used to jeans and a T-shirt.

"I should start dressing like this more often," he said to himself.

Ten minutes after he was dressed, Angelica stepped out of the bathroom. The business suit outlined her curvy features considerably. The shorter skirt looked very sexy on her, especially with the addition of the high heels.

"You look amazing," Ethan said, smiling.

"You don't look too bad yourself!"

Ethan went to the dresser and started to unplug his laptop. The screen had two words of importance on it: 'Virus Detected'. He hurriedly closed the internet browser and logged off the computer. Unplugging it from the wall, he placed it in his pack, along with his other belongings and they went out the door.

Putting the BMW into gear, Ethan headed towards the downtown industrial park. Angelica silently sat beside him in the passenger seat. They took the city streets instead of the freeway. Mixing in with the other cars would help conceal themselves better than being out in the open highway. It was a simple precaution; but a preventative measure nonetheless.

Taking a left onto Franklin Drive, Ethan noticed a man in a white convertible in the distant lane behind him. He had kept an eye on the rear view mirror since they had left. The car had been the only vehicle which had been behind them continuously. It's just my imagination; he thought to himself, I'm on edge. Those sick bastards couldn't *possibly* know where they were. He had left virtually no trail; he'd paid in cash; they had stayed at an unknown motel.

"What are you looking at," inquired Angelica.

"Nothing," he replied as he glanced at her, then back to the mirror, "I'm just keeping tabs on the road is all."

"Bullshit," she exclaimed.

"I want to make sure we're not being followed."

To ease his suspicions, Ethan turned right on the next street, and then right again. He remembered this from a movie he had seen. If the car *was* following them, it would take the same route they had. Sure enough, the man in the convertible turned as well.

Ethan slowed the car down to hit the red light so the man could catch up. The unknown gentleman pulled up to the side of the BMW and Ethan took a good look at him. The balding man looked back and flashed a friendly smile and waved to him through his open window.

"Hi there," he said.

The guy reminded him of his grade school science teacher. He was the epitome of a skinny computer nerd. He looked like a family man; plaid shirt, thick round glasses; even a bow tie. There were two small children in the back seat waving to him.

"Hi," Ethan replied, with a smile.

"*That's* the guy who's going to kill us," Angelica laughed.

"Shut up, Ange," Ethan groaned as he went through the green light.

The winding parking structure of Metacorp Laboratories was actually separate from the building itself. Ethan moved the car past the automated parking arm and halfway up the roundabout till he finally found an empty stall. He parked the car and they took the elevator down to the first floor entryway into the building.

The interior was magnificent. A large metallic sign bore the corporate name as they walked in. It was situated above a circling globe of the Earth. The smooth black marble of the walls reflected back the lights towards the center of the lobby, where a large reception desk was located. Security cameras were adorned across the ceiling while armed guards circled, like birds of prey. They watched the visitors closely.

Angelica nudged Ethan in the side.

"How the *hell* do you think we are going to get in there?"

"I'm not going to get us in," he replied, "*You* are."

Ethan walked up to the reception area and a guard approached them.

"Can I help you," asked the mousy lady behind the desk.

"We're here to see Doctor Armin Zolof."

"Do you have an appointment Sir?"

"Ma'am, we are here on behalf of the Taylor Foundation; this is Angelica Natash," Ethan said as he motioned for Angelica.

Ethan was hoping the ploy worked. The entire world knew of the distinguished Taylor Foundation as a center of prestige with a highly-regarded reputation. Metacorp was a Genetics Research facility, very much like the Taylor Foundation. Corporations like this; in this day and age, worked together and shared information all the time.

With a little luck, the receptionist would assume they were *supposed* to be here on some kind of research foray and just let them in.

It worked.

The lady looked up at Angelica in awe.

"Ms. Natash; I'm sorry," she stammered, "I didn't recognize you. I apologize for the inconvenience, but may I see your identification?"

"It's okay," Angelica replied, smoothing into her part, "Here you are."

The receptionist took a close look at the ID, and then motioned for a guard.

"Thank you. Sorry for the hassle, but it's procedure. I'll have Simonson escort you up."

"Thank you," said Ethan and led Angelica by the back towards the elevators.

The guard led them into the elevator and up to the sixth floor. According to the signage, the Doctor's office was on the second level, but the guard told them he was usually in the research facility. Stepping off the elevator, they walked into something out of a sci-fi novel.

The path leading to the lab was circular and lighted with blue bulbs. An electronic touch pad was at the further end and miniature security devices scanned the walkway from side to side. The guard pressed his thumb to the pad and the transparent silver doors opened up into an open zoo of various experimentation. In the middle of all the chaos, stood the frail-looking Doctor Armin Zolof, peering at them curiously.

"Zolof," said the guard," the lady and the gentleman are from the Taylor Foundation. They say you've been expecting them?"

Ethan clenched his fists, ready at a moment's notice, to take out the guard. He wondered if he had led them into a 'lion's den'.

Zolof looked at the guard and then back to Ethan and Angelica. Ethan noticed that he hesitated, ever so subtly.

"Yes, yes; thank you Simonson. I can handle things from here."

Ethan waited until the guard had left before he spoke. Zolof was still staring at him; no emotion showing.

"Doctor Zolof, my name is..."

Zolof cut him off immediately.

"I *know* who you are *D114*; or Ethan Swan; or whatever you are calling yourself these days."

"Listen, you..." Angelica started.

Zolof ignored her as he interrupted again.

"*Before* you threaten me with something *cliché*; I also *know* what you are capable of. As such, I did *not* inform the guard."

Ethan looked at him blankly for a moment.

"I came here for answers," he stated, "Why don't we start there."

"You want to know what you *are*, is that it?"

"For the moment; that will do."

Who *was* this man? Why did he act so nonchalant, giving up information so freely? He has no feeling, no remorse, nothing. He's empty inside. Is this what the devil has promised his servants?

"Are you *sure* you want to know this?"

"I didn't come this far for nothing, *Doctor*," Ethan said sarcastically.

Armin took a seat and motioned for them to sit down as well. Ethan wanted to reach out and wipe the look of disdain upon his face. He took a small breath and continued.

"We found you in a *Christian* orphanage of all places," the doctor spat, "you were just three months old. The perfect age for the Program; you had not been too exposed to the outside world as of yet. Your submersion in the Dep-med lasted for *six years*. Injections of Genome 6-66 were freely given at an accelerated pace. As you are aware, your genetic structure has been greatly enhanced; both in mind and body."

The doctor paused for a minute and smiled wickedly. He absently rolled up his sleeves. Strange markings decorated his arms in satanic verse.

"You were placed with your *Caretaker*, and watched over the years to determine your worthiness and dedication to becoming what you are *meant to be*."

"You mean my *father*," Ethan stated.

"Earl Swan was no father of yours, boy. He was *Illuminati*; like the rest of us. That worthless traitor was going to tell you *everything* before the time of *our* god's reconstitution upon this plane, and we could *not* have that."

"*You* killed my father," Ethan shouted, getting up from his seat. He spat at the withered old man.

The Doctor was visibly shaken for a moment, but recovered quickly. He put his hands up, and then motioned for Ethan to sit back down. Ethan stayed standing; anger swelling up in him.

"Not *I*; oh no – I am not *worthy* enough to hold that position. I am only a servant in the grand scheme of things. Even I am not told to *whom* that rite of passage belonged to. This is a secretive group; we have been in existence since the beginning. Even your so-called Jesus Christ was well aware of our power."

Angelica stood up as well. She grabbed Zolof by his arm and asked him a question.

"What do you mean by 'what he was meant to be'? Tell me!"

Zolof straightened in his chair and pushed her hand away before he began.

"The Illuminati was begun for two reasons: Wealth and Power. If you have these two things; you have something so much more: **Control**. Long ago, we set forth the motions to bring our god what he has been promised since his falling from the accursed plane of existence called Heaven; Armageddon! He *will* rule this world and we will be at his side! It is inevitable."

He looked at Angelica. Both Ethan and Angelica were listening intently.

"There are many world leaders that we have put into power for our own reasons. They are chosen by their faith to the Illuminati and their ability to obey. They are like cattle; leading the world into war and chaos."

He paused and smiled.

"*You* should know this my dear; after all, we could not let the people of Nabuhn start a holy crusade and bring about a revival of the disease, you call Christianity! You should have seen their faces; happily accepting their free inoculations of vaccines. Ha – we engineered it; the dola Virus! After all, we needed to bring down the *Christian* population count; they were simply a test!"

Angelica's jaw dropped as sadness swelled her eyes. The next minute, she was enraged. How can these...people have such little regard for human life? She went up to him and slapped him hard on his smiling face. The frail man recoiled in pain.

"You haven't answered my question," she screamed at him.

Armin shook his head and looked at them again, emotionless.

"*As* I was saying; the coming of the Antichrist has been foretold. However, the hierarchy of the Illuminati grew tired of waiting. With their wealth and knowledge of genetic engineering, they began to look for a suitable candidate in the hopes of *creating* the Antichrist."

"*This calls for wisdom: let him who has understanding reckon the number of the beast, for it is the name of a human person, its number is six hundred and sixty-six,*" Zolof quoted.

The doctor turned his head and stared at Ethan.

"Your bloodline reaches back to that of Judas Iscariot; the Great Betrayer of Christ. What better subject to choose than the ancestor of the man who was responsible, for killing God!"

It was Ethan's turn to go into shock. The statement had completely taken him off guard. His face turned a shade of white and his eyes flared with anger.

Zolof purposely paused for a moment; savoring the moment of revalation with great satisfaction.

Ethan sank back down into the chair, looking like a frightened deer, trapped in the headlights. Angelica moved to be closer to him and lightly touched his arm.

Ethan's mind worked furiously. He knew very well about Judas Iscariot; the *disciple* of Jesus Christ who had betrayed him for thirty pieces of silver. How can this be; he thought, his emotions running out of control. Was he destined for *evil*; *created* to *become* the Antichrist? Control; that's what they wanted; and control, he would give them; control over his own destiny. He focused back on Zolof.

The mad Doctor was laughing in his chair, as he stared at Ethan with those cold, dead eyes.

Ethan felt himself losing control. He got up, took Angelica by the hand, and headed for the doorway out of the lab.

"Don't worry young man," Zolof called after him, "I do *not* want to see you hurt. You still have *obligations* to fulfill; after all you are *my* creation!"

Ethan ignored the apparent jibe. He wanted to *kill* the man on the spot; however he knew that if he did that, he would lose what restraint he'd been trying to build. *They* would know that they had accomplished what they had set out to do. Instead, he would give him something to remember him by.

Ethan turned back and walked over to Zolof, leaving Angelica to ponder what he was about to do. He clenched his hand into a fist and struck.

"I have memories!"

The sudden impact hit Zolof like a hammer to his temple as his head twisted sharply to the side.

"I have hopes; I have dreams!"

The outbreak of wrath continued as fist upon fist struck the scientist. Tears clouded his vision until only the loud thuds of his punishment remained.

"I have love!"

Angelica could only watch as Ethan took his vengeance upon the battered old man. Breathing heavily, Ethan finally let up and turned towards her. He took by the arm and led her forward.

"I am no one's *creation*," he spat back, as he turned and walked out the door.

Taking the elevator back down to the lobby, Ethan was fuming. Everything he had just heard from Zolof was tearing at his mind.

Out of everything he had just been made aware of, the thing that hurt him incredibly was the fact that his *own* father had been part of the Illuminati! He didn't know how to feel about the man he had once loved and respected. In the end, it seemed as if his father had tried to do the right thing; but that did not negate the fact that he had known and allowed the Illuminati to influence Ethan's life, since the beginning! Further still; had Earl Swan known all along what they had done to him? Had he condoned it? Had he been part of it?

Was his ultimate destiny to become the embodiment of evil that was the Antichrist? Was he to turn this world upside down and cause it to burn? He could never bring himself to accept such a fate.

Angelica was trying to say something, but he didn't hear. He felt as if he were under water; aware of his surroundings, but unable to comprehend or communicate effectively. He sank back into his despair, unconsciously blocking her.

What of his relationship to the former disciple of Christ? He may as well have been related to the devil himself. Judas Iscariot; like his father, had tried to return the blood money he had accepted and do the right thing. Ultimately, he had hung himself; sentenced forevermore, to burn in hell for all eternity. Hell is what the Illuminati *wanted;* and *hell* is what he would give them!

Ethan suddenly felt a hard slap to the side of his head; accompanied by a stinging sensation. His surroundings focused back to his eyes. He was still in the elevator; Angelica looked like she was very worried.

"Listen to me," Angelica yelled, "I know this was something you were unprepared for; Christ, *that's* an understatement, with *what* you've just been told. I can't finish this alone, Ethan. You need to snap out of it!"

The elevator stopped and the doors opened back into the lobby. The light flooded in and he sobered up enough to move his body.

"We're going back to my father's estate," she continued, "No more lies; we need to tell him everything."

She grabbed him by the arm and pushed him out of the elevator and walked him down the hall.

"Is he alright Ma'am," questioned the receptionist, seeing Ethan's pale countenance.

"Yes; he's fine," Angelica replied, pulling Ethan towards the exit.

"Are you sure you don't want me to have Simonson escort you," pressed the lady behind the reception desk.

"I *said* we can manage."

Angelica opened the door, looking back to see the lady picking up the phone and dialing a number. She was suspicious; they had to hurry.

The clean fresh air helped Ethan to finally breathe normally. He regained his composure for a minute, and then ran to the make-shift garden on the side of the building. He emptied the contents of his stomach into the flowerbed. He stood up, wiped his mouth, and took a deep breath. The shock had apparently worn off; he was back in control.

Angelica looked at him in concern.

"I'm okay," he said, "Let's go."

They ran to the car in the parking garage and Ethan unlocked the BMW, to let them in. He put the car into reverse and backed up. They sped down the ramp and onto the street. He needed to get them back to Christoph's place. He looked back in the rear view mirror. No one followed them.

"They manipulated me too, Ethan," Angelica started, "I'm beginning to think the Illuminati have a hand to play in *all* the turmoil happening in this miserable world. Those sick bastards are *everywhere*; politicians; government officials; even presidents for all we know!"

"Their global, Ange; *we* can't get them all," Ethan said absently, "but the *unity* in people *can*. The world needs to *know*."

Ethan turned the car onto the on-ramp of the highway, almost hitting another vehicle.

"How can you say that; so *many* are a part of this? Haven't you ever wondered how we let ourselves…how humanity has *let* itself get caught up in this mess? "

Ethan let out a small laugh and shook his head knowingly.

"*Everybody* is for sale, Ange. Society has grown so wicked; *power* is their object of worship, not religion or God. Reverence for good will cease to exist. I understand now, what the Professor meant. We are *all born into sin*; we are easily corrupted by power and madness; but we have a *choice* if we want to continue down that path."

Angelica brought her head down as if she had given up on humanity altogether. How could normal, every-day people turn from God into the embrace of satan just like that?! How could they just give up their friends; their families; their souls?

"You're *wrong*, Ethan, some people don't have a *choice*," she replied solemnly.

"*Yes* they do, Ange," Ethan stated, "its called *free will!*"

CHAPTER VI – VENGEANCE

After some time, they finally came to Christoph's mansion. Ethan pulled the car up and then he and Angelica walked through the front door. The butler, Henry, greeted them at the door.

"Your father has been called by the Board to the Taylor Foundation. He has requested that you both remain here until he returns."

"Alright Henry," Angelica sighed, "We'll wait."

She led Ethan into the house and they retired to the living quarters. Angelica said she wanted to pick up a few things. Ethan sat down and waited for her in one of the comfortable couches. The only hope they had left was to somehow use Christoph's influence to make this public. The general population would have to be told.

He mindlessly fumbled through some old magazines on the table in front of him; stumbling upon one with a cover spread of the Taylor Foundation. It showed Christoph Natash standing in front of his company, along with some other important looking gentleman. The

Headline said 'Taylor Foundation adds yet another Corporation to its Portfolio'. He skimmed through the magazine and found the article.

'Billionaire Christoph Natash is a man of considerable prestige and power. He has started multiple corporations around the world, including the Taylor Foundation, here in the U.S. His surprising move to purchase the weapons manufacturer, Lucid Arms International has brought mixed reactions from officials of the European Government. Lucid Arms is the largest manufacturer of armaments in the country; importing and exporting to many foreign military institutions.

Natash; known for his considerable research into genetics and his many splinter companies, including Metacorp Laboratories and Gen-max...'

Ethan stopped dead in his reading. He went back and read it again just to make sure.

'...including *Metacorp* Laboratories and Gen-max...'

'My God," he exclaimed under his breath.

He noticed a shadow behind him and instinctively put his hand by his neck, knowing what was about to happen.

The garrote wire was blocked by his hand, as it struggled to tighten around his throat. The butler uttered no words; simply met his eyes, as Ethan turned his head back to gaze at his attacker. No emotion at all, Ethan noticed; just brute strength.

He planted both feet on the table before him and quickly pushed upwards with all his might. The couch tipped backwards, along with Henry. It gave him the opportunity of surprise as the big man's hands loosened his grip; enough for Ethan to break free of the deadly vise.

Ethan rolled away as the butler smoothly stood up in front of him. The man rolled up his sleeves, revealing the intricate tattoos on his arms. He then charged at his victim.

Ethan side-stepped away from the lunge and pushed his back with his palms, using the butler's own weight to propel him across the room. He crashed headfirst, into a showcase full of small ceramic statues and memorabilia. The broken glass cut his face with small lacerations, making him appear far more fearsome. Blood dripped from his shattered face, yet still he got back up and charged again.

Ethan met him head on, fists in a flurry of motion. Striking the large man with multiple blows, he pushed him back a few feet. Still silent and knowing he faced an opponent much more than human, Henry reached behind his coat and pulled out a semi-automatic pistol. He pointed it at Ethan and smiled.

"I have a problem with *guns*," Ethan stated, as he swiftly took out the man's leg with a crouched swipe of his foot.

"*I don't*," cried Angelica, as she pulled the trigger of the weapon she was holding.

The gun went off loudly as two bullets entered the butler's head; brain matter exploding in a sickly display of shattered bone and flesh. Angelica came running to Ethan and helped him up. She did not show the slightest of fear.

"Are you okay," she asked, excitedly.

"Better than he's going to be," he answered, as he took the gun slowly from her hands, "Are you?"

"These people deserve to die," she said without hesitating.

"And your *father*," Ethan asked.

"What does *he* have to do with this?"

Ethan walked over to the table, picked up the magazine, and handed it to her.

"He is *Illuminati*, Ange," he stated, showing her the article. She quickly skimmed through it and threw it down in exasperation.

"It has to be coincidence! Ethan…please"

He felt her pain and anger as he looked into her tear-filled eyes. There was nothing he could do to console her from the truth.

"*None of this has been coincidence*. Metacorp, Ange, he's involved in all of this. He's been buying time."

After recovering from her initial shock, Angelica took a seat on the remaining couch. She sat there, slowly shaking her head. Ethan came up to her and put his arms around her shoulders. He knelt before her and peered into her eyes.

"He brought Zolof in, once he took control of Metacorp; think about it."

"I'm not arguing with you; it's just…"

Angelica hugged Ethan and cried into his arms. Thirty minutes later, she let him go.

"Where did you get this gun," Ethan questioned, as he palmed the weapon.

"I was in the military, remember," she replied and paused, "Ethan, what are we going to do?"

"We cut the *head* from the body. We go the Taylor Foundation."

He handed her back the gun.

"Keep this; we may have need of it."

Angelica put it into her purse and they walked out of the estate, hand in hand. Ethan unlocked the trunk of his car and pulled out the Khukuri blades. He put them both into his belt and put on a dark coat he took from the car. They pulled out and headed for the Taylor Foundation.

The Taylor Foundation consisted of twin tower buildings; each of the immense structures rising up towards the sky had thirty-three floors. The buildings were solidly built, with open glass panes showing the various offices of those who resided there. The first tower was the one they were headed for.

Neither he nor Angelica said a word; both lost in thought at the imminent confrontation that was going to happen. The tension they both felt was unsaid.

Walking through the swivel doors, Ethan was awed at the magnificence of the complex. Smooth elegant ceilings rose up at least twelve feet high, prominently displaying the modernistic architecture. A giant screen loomed up from the Italian tiled flooring, showing advertising for new advancements in genetics that the corporation had undertaken. Exquisite marble statues and paintings were scattered in front of the ever-expanding crème-colored walls.

No one bothered to stop or question them, as they made their way through the maze of hallways and took a lift to the twenty-second floor. Everyone recognized Angelica as Christoph Natash's daughter and allowed them to proceed undeterred.

Angelia knew exactly where she was going; obviously she had visited Natash multiple times over the course of her upbringing. She finally led Ethan towards a large office with fancy glass doors. A handsome young man in a beige business suit passed by and stopped Angelica. Ethan was on edge, his hand fingering the cold of the blade.

"Angelica, so good to see you," he said as he offered up his hand, "Your father is in a board room meeting; he has asked that no one disturb him, but he should be back here in an hour, if you'd care to wait?"

"I'll see myself in, Hank," she replied as she shook his hand, "Thanks."

Ethan breathed a sigh of relief.

She opened the doors and Ethan walked in, as he made sure both blades were snug on his side. The office was empty as expected. Bits of a red and black waxy substance were visible on the floor forming a large circle of some sort. He rubbed it between his fingers. It felt like candle wax.

Ethan stood up and observed the enormous bay window, peering down, into the traffic below.

He walked up to it and took in the view. It was breathtaking. The man had all this, he thought to himself, and still it wasn't enough.

"It's beautiful, isn't it," Angelica's voice broke through the silence, from behind him, "I used to just sit up here and watch all the people walking from place to place. My father would sit at his desk barking orders and my brother…"

Ethan turned to look at her. She just broke into tears. He felt lost.

"I'm sorry, Ange," he said.

"So am I," she replied, obviously in distress.

Ethan acknowledged her with a nod and walked towards the desk in the corner of the office. Angelica followed.

He became aware of a small file cabinet, hidden under the wing of the large table and bent down to peer at it. It had an electronic lock with a digital face panel. There were numbers on the top of it, much like a telephone. He thought for a minute, and then pushed four numbers: 2-0-1-2 and the lock opened immediately.

He rifled through the folders that were marked. He reached in and took out a thick folder labeled 'D114'. He looked through the papers carefully. They contained a lot of information about him; the day he was born; his past achievements; school transcripts; copies of his medical records; digital photographs.

Each page was marked on the bottom corner: TFCN. Of course, he thought – Taylor Foundation; Christoph Natash. He cursed himself for not being more observant. Angelica stared down at the papers from beside him in disbelief.

"He's been keeping tabs on you; throughout your *entire life!*"

Ethan didn't respond. He pulled out some more documents and spread them across the expansive desk. They had various statistics written on them.

-11 Year Developmental Stage: Subject has shown remarkable adaptation in both mental and physical performance - However, violent outbreaks continue to be frequent.

-16 Year Developmental Stage: Programming halted until full maturity is obtained.

-19 Year Developmental Stage: Subject continues to refuse Subliminal Stimulation.

-22 Year Developmental Stage: Subject will be closely observed to determine his capacity for re-programming.

-23 Year Developmental Stage: Subject scheduled for termination; mental blocks have been breached.

Authorization: TFCN

"That son of a bitch," Ethan screamed, as he threw Christoph Natash's glass name-plate at the long mirror by the side wall.

It crashed into the mirror, sending fragments of sharp glass flying all over. The name-plate landed upside down on the floor below. Reflected into the mirror, Ethan looked closely at the letters. If he read it backwards, the letters spelled out: S-A-T-A-N-H. Without the silent 'H' in his name, it appeared to say SATAN.

'That's not going to help,' Angelica said.

"Ange, let me see your phone," he asked, ignoring her protests.

She gave it to him and he dialed a number. The phone rang a few times and Christoph Natash answered on the other end.

"Hello Sweetheart," began his voice, "Are you on your way home? I can't talk long; I have someone in my office."

"I highly doubt that," answered Ethan.

"Ethan?"

"Yes, it's me *Uncle* Christoph."

"Ethan; why would you say that," he asked inquisitively.

"…Because Angelica and I are the *only* ones, here in your *office*."

Ethan hung up the phone and gazed at Angelica. He did not know what was to be expected, but he'd had enough of waiting for all these horrors to happen to him and to those he loved.

"We don't have long," he stated, taking out both Khukuri blades from his sides.

"Ethan…I don't know if I can do this," Angelica said nervously.

The doors opened and Christoph Natash stepped into the office. Behind him, was the man in plaid who had been following them before in the white convertible.

Ethan looked over at Angelica.

"You can apologize later."

Christoph Natash surveyed the room, silently taking in the documents scattered on his desktop. The gentleman who was with him took off his shirt and his glasses, and then calmly pulled out a Khukuri knife from behind his belt.

The man was exceptionally muscular for his size. He was naked underneath except for the elaborate tattoos that outlined his upper torso. A large red pentacle formed the majority of the tattoo; the top two points, formed into spiraling horns. The spaces between the upper triangles containing three numbers: 6-6-6. On his belly, the same date of the Mayan's divination of doomsday was inscribed in jagged numbers: 2-0-1-2, as if they had been carved in by a jagged blade.

Christoph shook his head slowly, staring back at the two. He remained unflustered.

"I'd heard you made a recent trip to see the good Doctor Zolof."

"He had some *interesting* things to say," Ethan replied back, watching them closely.

"Angelica," Christoph nodded to his daughter.

"You *disgust* me, you twisted fuck," she spat.

"*That* is a matter of opinion," he replied, smiling.

Angelica reached into her purse and pulled forth the revolver, aiming it directly at her father.

"If you shoot that in here; you will be gunned down by my security," he said calmly.

"Put it away, Ange," Ethan said.

She looked confused, but complied with his request. The old man turned his attention towards Ethan.

"People have lost faith, Ethan; in themselves and in God. They are easily and willingly led astray; straight to the *gates of hell.* The Illuminati has *always* known this; it was foretold. We are only ushering in the inevitable; the *New Dawn* of mankind. Look at the world today; it is what they *want!*"

The bastard did not even think to deny any of this. He simply did not care nor was he stalling for time. He believed in what he did.

"Not me, Christoph; *not everyone,*" Ethan replied, "You created me to become your tool for Armageddon; you wanted me to bring destruction to this world. You disregarded my *free will.*"

"It's not too late for you, Ethan. You, my boy, are the ultimate specimen in *human evolution; you* are the instrument of this world's decimation! Of course, you are *so much more* than that. The entire world will bow down at your feet. You will be a *leader* amongst men. You *are our* Antichrist!"

The strange man moved slowly; circling Ethan and Angelica. Ethan restrained his urge to fight, all the while keeping him in sight. He wanted more information first.

"How could you do this Christoph; you were the *only* family I had left! I…"

"The Illuminati only accepts those that are willing to sacrifice *whatever it takes*, to beget the rightful rule of Lucifer! It is *more* than just a pledge; it is life, freely given to the *Morning Son*. My ancestors were among the chosen few, selected to *lead* the Illuminati towards the new age."

Christoph paused as he took a few steps towards him.

"It is a facade, Ethan! These people that you *run* to protect; do you really believe that they do not *deserve* the worst? The wife-beater or child molester who goes to Church for the sole reason that they feel they *must*; not because they *want* to. How about the countless people who attend services for the *same* reason, only to go out into the world and treat others with disdain and disgust; the pastors who dress in fancy suits and ask for donations while molesting children! *These* are the sheep you would fight for?"

Ethan felt his blood beginning to boil.

"Maybe so, Christoph; but there are others who *have* faith; there are *those who will not* allow the Illuminati to force its *reign* on them! As for the *rest* of mankind; they can decide for themselves."

Christoph stared at them and laughed. He motioned something to the other man.

"Your programming is *not* yet complete, but if you slit her throat," he said, motioning towards Angelica, "you would have *proven* to us that you are still the rightful *heir* of this world!"

"She's your daughter, Christoph; your blood!"

"The blood of those who we hold most dear is a dutiful sacrifice that we must make! It matters not; she will be exalted in infamy throughout the Illuminati for giving her life to the only true cause. Like Tyler, before her has done!"

Angelica looked at her father with utter disgust.

"You *killed* my brother," she questioned angrily, "Your *own son*?!"

"I was required to take leadership; a *small* sacrifice for the dark god, my dear," he replied, smiling.

Angelica withdrew the gun from her purse and pointed it at her father.

This sick, semblance of a man would actually *murder* his own daughter, Ethan thought. He would do this simply to keep his status as the leader in a satanic cult; whose only purpose was to bring about death and ruin? He would kill her in cold blood and feel no remorse whatsoever.

Ethan felt the rage swell up in him, and *this* time, he let it take over. His restraint *snapped* like a flimsy rubber band.

Twirling the blades in his hands, he looked around for the strange, tattooed man. Christoph saw the anger in Ethan's face and tried to make a move. Angelica cocked the gun she was pointing and he stopped in his tracks. She waited patiently.

"Gregor," Christoph shouted in the man's direction, "destroy the whelp and Lucifer will *embrace* you with his power!"

Ethan and the tattooed man rushed each other at the same time. Ethan went down on one knee and ducked under the swipe of his blade. Knife up and outward, he slashed Gregor across his arm, and then came up with an elbow to the side of his face.

Gregor backed up a little, looked at the blood and shrugged it off, as though it were merely a paper cut. He came forward, knife up in the air and stabbed downwards.

Ethan blocked with one of the blades, and used the other one to thrust downwards, taking off the man's ear. He kicked his foot into the side of the man's calf to get him off balance. He then quickly used the same foot to strike the middle shin of his calf.

Gregor flew back and landed on his back. In an instant, he flipped his body back up again, knife waving dangerously. Blood shot out from the injured side of his head, but he just smiled wickedly.

Nothing seems to faze this guy, Ethan thought, he just keeps coming. What are these people?

Gregor leapt at Ethan, twisting his body to avoid the razor sharp swipes, and hit the blade from Ethan's hand. The strange man kicked him in the stomach. Ethan doubled back in pain and was forced to jump back, narrowly avoiding an incoming thrust.

They were now on either sides of the office, facing each other with unbridled fury. The man had Ethan's other knife.

Gregor looked at him, and then pulled back and threw the blade towards him. The sharp instrument sliced through the air, as Ethan pulled his upper body backwards. In one continuous motion, he used his other hand to reach out and grab the handle from mid-air, and then flipped his body to the right. He landed, once again with both blades in his hands. He beckoned with his hand for the man to come towards him.

The tattooed man stared at him in awe. For once, he wavered and the look on his face showed that his confidence was slowly draining. He faced someone that actually frightened him.

Glancing over at Angelica, Ethan saw that she had things under control. Christoph was planted firmly in the same spot, not daring to move. His countenance had greatly paled.

"Do *not* fail *me*, Gregor," Christoph warned.

Gregor slightly nodded his head in understanding and rushed Ethan again. Ethan stepped sideways and struck him in the gut with a powerful kick. The pained man swung his arm in a swift motion and managed to slice Ethan along the leg. Ethan limped backwards in pain. Gregor took this opportunity to smash Ethan in the face with his free hand. He jumped onto the office desk and appeared to be getting into position to leap from it, knife hand outstretched.

Ethan recovered instantly and ran the few steps towards Gregor. He swung his leg above the desk, taking out Gregor's footing. Gregor tried to turn his body, only to fall back first towards the ground.

As he was in mid-fall, Ethan turned his body and brought both blades down into the tattooed man's chest. Blood spurted forth as Gregor closed his eyes for the final time. As he hit the floor, with a thud, his body's last death spasms came and went.

Blades still buried in the man's torso, Ethan turned his blood-spattered face to look at Christoph. The once haughty man was now slightly quivering in his shoes. His eyes, however, betrayed no sign of lost confidence. Ethan pulled the blades from the dead man, stood up, and walked towards Christoph.

"What do *you* think you are going to do," Christoph asked, mockingly, "You are just a *failed experiment*; nothing more! I *own* the police; do you think *they* or the other members of the *Illuminati* will allow you to live?"

"I have your files, Christoph; names; numbers; everything I need. It would be a shame if it got into the wrong hands. I'm *sure* the rest of your cult will leave me in peace. I, on the other hand, have my *own* plans for *them*."

"My…my security…they will not allow you to hurt me! You cannot kill me."

"I'm not going to kill you, Christoph; you're going to kill *yourself*."

Ethan took the old man's hands and wrapped them around the hilts of the blades. He faced the sharp, pointed edges upwards. Christoph looked at Angelica, pleadingly.

"Angelica," he said.

"Fuck you and *die*," she replied as she spat on him. She turned her back to him.

"Ethan…Ethan; don't do this! You *belong with me*!"

"You may be right Christoph; then I'll *see you in hell!*"

Ethan took a hold of both his hands and brought them upwards with such force that the tips of the Khukuri knives went through the bottom of Christoph's jaw, and then came up through the top of his head. Gurgling blood spilled from his mouth as the leader of the Illuminati collapsed in a heap on the dirty floor.

Ethan stood up and gently led Angelica by the arm towards Christoph's desk. There, he pulled and yanked on the hidden file draw until it gave. He put his coat over it and went to the small bathroom in the office and grabbed some paper toweling.

Angelica walked over and picked up the file draw underneath the coat, and then looked at Ethan.

"What are we going to do now," she asked.

Ethan walked up to her, held her in his arms, and then looked into her eyes.

"I'm going to *kill them all; one by one.*"

Epilogue:

It was a rainy night; the weather steadily getting worse. Lightening struck a tree in the thick of the forest, bringing it down into the leading path of Midland Trail. Thunder crackled loudly in the night sky. The neighing of horses could be heard in the distance.

It was dark in the ranch house. The only light inside, was the dancing reflections cast by the red and black candles along the floor. The stench of congealed blood came from the main quarters.

William Hicks filled a black kettle with water and placed it on the heated stove. A wet red handprint left its mark on the handle. He stepped to the white porcelain sink and washed his bloodied hands. The crimson flood went down the drain like a small whirlpool.

Hicks smiled at his reflection in the small mirror above the kitchen sink. His mind swirled with recent events. The poor fool had gotten himself lost while hiking in the woods that night. He had blindly run through the forest, only to find himself at the horse ranch. He didn't realize that the pounding rain washed away his footprints, as he knocked at the door for help. That was his final mistake.

Will's cell phone rang at his side.

"Hello?"

"Will, this is *Ethan Swan*."

"Ethan…"

Will paused and let out a strangled cough.

"E…Ethan; how…are you? I…I was worried when you didn't show. Is everything…alright?"

"I'm just fine Will. I wanted to come by and thank you for everything you've done for Angelica and I."

"I…I don't know if that's a good idea. My wife…she's sick. She's not feeling well and I… just got back home."

"No, you didn't."

"What? Why…why do you say that?"

There was only silence on the other end. Thunder rumbled in the distance.

"Hello…Ethan?"

No answer came forth.

"Hello?"

The rain beat down rapidly against the window.
Will reached for the off button as the phone
crackled back to life.

"Will…"

"Wh…What?"

"Your water's boiling."

William Hicks threw down the phone.
Panicking with fear, he turned to run. He didn't
even feel the long blade as it was thrust into his
heart. Blood spilt as his scream was drowned by
the sharp whistling of the kettle.

END?

WWW.MORNINGSON.INFO

THE TRUTH AWAITS THOSE WHO SEEK IT……

CLOSING:

If you liked this book...or didn't; please feel free to email me with your comments and feedback: ContactUs@morningson.info

AUTHOR:

Nishan Kumaraperu was born in Colombo, Sri Lanka on April 10th, 1974. He grew up in England and the United States. He currently resides in Appleton Wisconsin with his wife, their five children, and two dogs.

He has always been a storyteller. All throughout his schooling years, he would write short stories of fantasy, sci-fi, and action adventure. During this time, he and a few friends would each write pieces of a story and exchange them to finish what the other had started. They would then share the final story amongst themselves and critique each other to the best of their abilities.

Kumaraperu's life was based on learning everything he was interested in. He gained valuable knowledge in multiple fields: Behavioral Counseling, Real Estate, Property Management, Technology, Finance, and even Cooking. He co-wrote his first screenplay with a friend using Final Draft. Since then, he has written his own screenplay and this Novel. For the past many years, he is the President and CEO of a computer corporation (CNR Enterprises / Elite I.T.) in Appleton Wisconsin.

He has written multiple articles for magazines and online journals, including being an Expert Author on Ezinearticles.com. Writing has always played an important part of his life since he was young and will always continue to be so.

**THE BATTLE FOR YOUR SOUL DOES NOT END HERE…

~Dedicated to my wife, Sarah and my wonderful children: Ethan, Cyerra, Cain, Sydney, & Ashlynn — I love you guys!

-THE MAYAN CALENDAR

-THE ALL SEEING EYE ON THE
DOLLAR BILL

-ARE YOU IN CONTROL?

ISBN: 978-0-615-27176-7

Library of Congress Control Number: 2009900197

www.ingramcontent.com/pod-product-compliance
Lightning Source LLC
Chambersburg PA
CBHW070841120626
46556CB00002B/834